BOOMERANG

BARRY HANNAH

BOOMERANG

HOUGHTON MIFFLIN / SEYMOUR LAWRENCE

Boston 1989

For information about permission to reproduce selections from this book, write to Permissions, Houghton Mifflin Company, 2 Park Street, Boston, Massachusetts 02108.

This novel is a work of fiction. Names, characters, places, and incidents either are the product of the author's imagination or are used fictiously.

Library of Congress Cataloging-in-Publication Data

Hannah, Barry.
Boomerang / Barry Hannah.
p.   cm.
ISBN 0-395-48882-6
I. Title.
PS3558.A476B66   1989   88-36881
813'.54—dc19   CIP

PRINTED IN THE UNITED STATES OF AMERICA

Q 10 9 8 7 6 5 4 3 2 1

The author would like to express his thanks to the University of Mississippi English Department, whose summer grant made the writing of *Boomerang* happier and more confident.

FOR DAVID MARION HOLMAN

1951–1988

AND FOR MY WIFE SUSAN

BOOMERANG

TINY

We were such tiny people in the Quisenberrys' pecan orchard.

We were so tiny but we were sincere. The Quisenberrys' house looked like a showboat on the Mississippi River, and when we were tiny we fought and we had secret intrigues. We built a fort out of railroad ties. The kids would roam out and find pecans and horse apples and a stick of dynamite.

There were Reds and Nazis out there.

We knew about dynamite. We once announced a rule that you couldn't come back to the fort unless you had something wonderful to tell. Our fort was very private.

We threw walnuts at each other. The Stovalls had a walnut grove. One night I was running around even more than usual. Mrs. Mell and her daughter Moochie tried to make me slow down. Moochie pulled down her pants and said, I'll show you mine if you'll show me yours. What a wonderful night that was, near the Stovalls' fishpond. It was a concrete pond with goldfish and big lily pads in it. But nothing would slow me down. Moochie's mother was a beautiful woman who worked in the drugstore. Mrs. Mell was the most beautiful woman I could imagine, outside of my aunts, Bertha and Bernice.

In my back yard Tommy Poates was in an Admiral television box moving slowly ahead, attacking the rest of us with an automatic rubber gun. Rod Flagler had brought in the idea of the automatic rubber gun from Culver City, California. The television box was as large as a refrigerator. Every time we ran up close, we got stung. We all dressed in short pants and nothing else. Fairly soon we learned not to get stung. Edward Ratliff set the box on fire with lighter fluid. It was quite amazing to see Tommy get out of the flaming box. Darn it, I'd never thought of that.

Preacher's kids lived in the barracks below us. Later I heard they were so poor they had to eat cold cereal for lunch. We fought them too. And hated them. All those preacher's kids were good athletes. They were never in the band, they were horrible skinny people with bad complexions. That's not true. That's a hideous statement. They were good and swift. And they were mean. We fought them with mudballs and threw cane spears at them. They were down there beyond the tall cane patch and they had nothing to eat and we were glad.

But one afternoon in Clinton I was standing out in the back yard of Edward Ratliff's house, helping him mow the tremendous acre of his yard. I was standing there in my shorts and bare chest. I thought I'd been stung by a hornet, but looked at my stomach and saw I'd been hit by a shot from an air rifle. The preacher's kids were giggling through the bushes. My god, they were all across the fence, laughing. I had no weapons on me. I was stupefied. All I could find near me was the boomerang I ordered out of the back of a comic book, $1.98. It took a couple weeks to save the dough. I went and got the boomerang and knelt over and pulled it out of the grass. There was nothing to do with it. There were bushes between us and the stormwire fence. There were plum trees and standing corn between me and the fellow who shot me. A lot of honeysuckle too. I looked over there and heard two of them giggling. The red welt on my belly was growing and still smarted terribly. When I threw the boomerang it went very high over them and then made a lovely twist, coming back. It just made it back to the Ratliffs' lawn. Maybe the guys never saw it, but it was a nice toss. I was learning to control it. It would almost come back to you, as promised in the ad. It would sail and then make a little return. Back into the St. Augustine grass. The preacher's kids would never have a lawn of St. Augustine grass.

They would never have anything except themselves and their air rifles, I thought. God, how I hated them.

But they were good. When we bought our own air rifles, they were ready. We had Daisys and we were out there behind the trees in the great pecan orchard. We had on plastic glasses too. What I mean is that two out of our six had on plastic glasses. The preacher's kids were behind the cane patch, all ganged up, shooting their air rifles at us. Even I knew this was dumb. They had three air rifles and we had six. We were moving up and getting behind the big trees so nothing could hit us. But everybody was chicken about being hit by beebees. I did not become the Pfc or the Sergeant at this point. I had my plastic glasses and my leather coat. Then I went into the meadow on my knees and started firing my Daisy over and over. Far in the back was Ratliff with his pellet gun that would penetrate a squirrel, but I wanted this to be a fair fight and I waved him back.

I received fire. All of them were shooting at me. But I was not being harmed. I caught a beebee in my right eyepiece. Moved ahead. Then the others came up. We had six guns to their three. So we started moving on them very slowly. They were out of beebees. Then we began moving very fast. They were in the back of the cane but then they fled.

I saw the boy who had shot me and started running after him. He had no shirt on and very thin blond legs. He was racing away toward his miserable barracks apartment and I aimed and shot him in the back. He went in the bottom apartment, howling with pain. I wanted to shoot him again. I shot him in the legs. I could hear him running on the stairs. And then he slammed the door. I gave it up when I heard his mother shriek.

Out there in September with the sun getting colder, in the gravel parking lot, looking at the stained yellow asbestos shingles where he lived, I took off my goggles. Thank god, I said to myself, I'm not him.

Later on I met David Bass, one of the preacher's kids, in Square Books here in Oxford. He smiled and said, Remember me? Certainly I did. He was older but he was still smiling, looking a little ragged around the eyes. He was coaching a ball team in Mississippi somewhere. I forget the town.

He was the fastest football player on the junior high team. You just handed him the ball and he would run away from everybody. He would go by the grasping end and then flee through the helpless linebackers down the field. We beat some teams 77–0 when I was the tiny quarterback, throwing over the taller boys to David Bass or Henry O'Neill. We took everybody. My head was always too little for my big plastic white helmet.

But we were the Clinton Arrows, not to be messed with.

An old man came off the sidelines to congratulate me one afternoon.

I was all sweaty in my white and red uniform. He hobbled up beside me and wanted to take my hand. I was nothing. I was five foot one. He told me I was the best passer he'd ever seen. The truth was I was so tiny I lateraled or handed off or threw it. I didn't like big people tackling me. I knew I had no future in athletics. I was going into music and my own poems. Quisenberry was second-string quarterback. But he was eating a lot of protein food and taking the weight course from Joe Weider. I gave the ball to him for the history of the Clinton Arrow football team. Eventually he broke all the records.

❑ ❑

Then there was a new guy came in our class named Horace Newcomb. He could recite "The Wreck of the Hesperus" cold, standing up in the class. My whole future life opened up when I heard him do that. What a thing to be able to do in junior high, I thought. What a showoff. Newcomb was tall and had hornrim glasses. In the band he played tuba. I was on cornet. Wyatt Newman was on viola, not with the band but over in Jackson with the symphony. I'd never heard of the instrument. In the band he played tuba also. The big guys in the band played tuba. Art Lee played cornet. William Quisenberry played clarinet. John Quisenberry played cornet, though he was becoming more the star quarterback. Then there was Joe Brown, a clear genius from Union, Miss. He was pale—thin, too. His arms were like the limbs of a mimosa. His forehead was high and he already knew about botany.

OXFORD

There is a tall black man walking slowly through the alleys of this town, wearing glasses. He goes slowly. You would never think he was looking for anything especially. But he has the big plastic bag. He's looking for beer cans. Next to him is a slim young German shepherd on a rope, a dog with blue eyes, trotting alongside. They must be fine friends. The man walks with difficulty. He has a cane. He has gray hair. He must be sixty. The dog is young and steps delicately around the pavement and the grass. The man has dignity. He does not want your pity. His beloved dog prances back and forth around him, helping him scent the beer cans. This is a college town and the beer cans lie everywhere. I believe he might get a penny apiece for them at the recycling plant.

❏ ❏

An overprivileged young man from Kentucky killed his girlfriend. He strangled her and left her in the room, passed out, then awoke to find something wrong. Awoke to the horror of himself. His attitude was the same as that of many rich spoiled kids at the university: Don't get in my way. They throw the beer cans everywhere so the tall black dignified man can make a living.

The jury gave the young man life. His Kentucky parents were horrified. They hired a bodyguard for him at Parchman so that the criminals wouldn't sodomize him like he did the girl, who told my nephew once she'd smoked dope every day since she was thirteen. No drugs were mentioned in the trial, although everybody knew drugs were involved. My son was in class with the killer. He brought his helmet into class, from his motorcycle, said my son.

My son they call the best guitarist in north Mississippi.

He neither smokes nor drinks. What a great improvement over me. He just stands up there and plays. As if nothing ever happened but his guitar, as if there were no history beyond himself. He doesn't know how to fight. Like our little Lhasa apso dog, Joscph, he just wasn't trained that way. In fact he has prevented me from violence several times.

❑ ❑

When I came to this town I was homesick after twenty years away from my home state. My hometown is three hours from here but this place was close enough. I had been on my last frightening flight to space, and I returned my rank to the pool. At the last I even poured my last little half vial of coke down the toilet.

I was here as a bachelor, and then my son joined me to go to the college.

The sun comes up like a purple diamond. The wet smoke in the air falls away, and there is the country. When you are meeting your next wife the house smells like charred embers and it's a two-story cottage with dry grass and the croquet tour you'd set out for your other two kids, Ted and Lee. There are a number of things here under the big blue long-clouded sky. Mainly there is music. My kids are all crazy about music. They come in with their tapes and their albums.

Right behind us they were grinding out a field to plant. I was paying $300 a month for privacy and then all the Muchles come here ripping up my back yard. I felt like a tenant farmer. Certain people don't care what they do to you as long as they are making a buck. What landlords.

I saw my future wife and declared my love at the Hoka. I was not doing too well. In depression I had spray-painted my kitchen and my car silver. I was wearing swimming trunks and a herringbone sports jacket. She was sitting with friends in a corner booth. I was trying to get some food down, so I ordered a salad, but I was eating it with my hands, she says. She was sitting there with her regal blond hair and her big gray eyes. I never even noticed her friends. We met them later but I had no idea who they were. The Hoka is an old warehouse made into a bohemian café with a movie house in the other half. Ron Shapiro, from St. Louis, owns and runs it. He works with a partner named Jim Dees. Dees begged my future wife to come over and sit with me, after I'd begged him to do it. I told her I had a plane and a boat, total lies. I asked her to marry me. All I asked was that she be rich and have a covered garage. She was not only poor but she was less than zero. When I got back on my feet I was in her kitchen and saw her pouring ketchup from one of those large cafeteria-sized jars. I almost broke down and cried for her poverty. She had two teenaged children and they didn't know what was happening with me in the house, having been on their couch for three days.

⊓ ⊓

The man leans on his cane to pick up a can.

He could be a professor. He looks like a man floating on serene thoughts after his immense history of thinking and deciding. He moves along slowly, no hurry. It's just money, it's just pennies, it's just to get by. My own old man moves along with a cane now, at eighty-four. He has a cancer — a big tumor off the bone near the spleen. But it's in control, after his neutron treatments in Houston, and the old man still walks along slowly, looking at the mysteries on the side of the road.

Where does the old black man live? What does he eat? What does the dog do at the home? Does it stay inside with him or sleep outside near the steps? Does the old black man ever read the newspapers?

I don't want to know, really.

I asked about him one afternoon, from Ollie Caruthers. I was sorry I asked. Ollie told me the old man carries a loaded .25 in his back pocket all the time. Maybe that's why he always looks so serene and philosophical. Lately he got brushed by a car, walking along some road looking for beer cans. He got laid up. I wanted to take him some food and offer my respects. But since I heard about the .25 I don't anymore. He's just as scared as the rest of us. I'm terribly sorry to hear it.

❑ ❑

A dude with no hopes, no prospects, alcoholic, twenty-four, eighth-grade dropout, white, got a divorce. He found a job taking care of the dogs at the animal shelter. I bought him a car and he started loving the dogs. He had ten of his own back at his mother's house, where he was staying now, though many nights he slept in the little Subaru. Then he quit the dog shelter because of personal differences with everybody. He simply left the place without telling anybody. He left dying puppies out in their own manure. He couldn't stand the women of the Humane Society. I have to hold it in because I'm president of the Humane Society now. All the women are sighing martyrs. They don't know how sighing they are, bossy and sometimes insane. But I am full of error myself.

❑ ❑

Wondering about the lady—eighty-four—who hardly ever leaves her kitchen. There is nothing in the town that interests her anymore. The old brick streets and the "old town," as they call it—Clinton, Mississippi—have been surrounded by subdivisions and the increasing Baptist church, with its ugly red bricks. There is an evangelism that reaches to Southeast Asia and heals the diseases of the natives and gives them hope itself, beyond their fatalism. The money is given from the purses of the old women and their reluctant husbands. Churches with their stacked bricks claiming all the view where there used to be great oaks and calm green meadows. The town has almost been changed into an asphalt maze running between two-story rectangles. She has no more interest in the town except for the mail she receives at the post office. She taught me modern poetry. Her husband, long dead now, taught me History of Civilization — an ambitious course, but he taught it to me. He'd been a war correspondent in World War One. He taught me about Spain and North Africa. He taught me about Paris and Germany. He taught me about China. He had a stiff posture and he wore nice long-collared shirts we heard were made in London.

That was when Mississippi College was good.

That was when J. Edgar Simmons was there.

That was when Louis Dollarship gave me praise.

That was when Annabell Jenkins was the prima donna of the eighteenth century.

That was when Tom Boswell taught a great class in Roman Ritual and Religion and we went over to his apartment and had pizza and beer afterward.

□ □

When we went out fishing, big cottonmouth moccasins were everywhere in the ponds and the lakes. Russell Williams and I were fishing in a boat on Lake Garaway. There was a snake lying on a little limb just this side of a big log. Russell threw over the log, where he let the "wounded minnow" — a topwater plug with spinners — lie so as to attract an enormous bass. He jerked the line softly a couple of times. Then the snake coiled up around the plug. Russell jerked it and he had him. He reeled it in. Snakes are harmless creatures, they say — yeah.

Now that I'm an adult they don't mess with me so much. You take a .410 shotgun and blow their heads off. They sure messed with you when you were a kid. Jim Harrison saw one wounded in the tail and it bit itself over and over. Shoot, shoot, shoot, is what I say.

UNCLES

A few weeks ago old Uncle Babe comes in with his cane. He can't sit in the sun because, he says, he's had forty skin cancers removed in the last couple of years. My old man asked him how his old friends were doing.

"They're all half dead," said Uncle Babe.

He was going back to his bedroom and my mother asked him what he had to say.

"Damn," he said.

"Well, that's not nice," said my mother, a deep Baptist lady. Uncle Babe has vicious arthritis.

I put up his shirts and pants in the closet and set his grip-bag on the cedar chest. He was sleeping in that high bed I slept in all through my teenage years. Outside the window were the oak trees, all bare now in the late warming month of March. There was the clayey ground on which no grass would ever grow. I'd mowed and raked this yard hundreds of times. I knew every inch of it like the back of my hand, from the St. Augustine grass in the front to the patches of ivy in the very back. I was a mad boy, angry about everything except my trumpet, which I played out of the open windows of my bedroom. I'd play in the air and try to make something happen in vacant air. Rafael Mendez was my idol. I tried to play the whole Arban book. My notes pierced out in the air with a sweet revenge on reality. The neighbors were kind not to complain. I was quite a howling, stumbling attack of sound. I dreamed long trumpet sounds and made my tone as sweet as possible.

In the last days of being swift and tiny, I recall raking the leaves and running the mower, increasing my muscles and taking a sweat break while the teenaged girls circled my house with their new driver's licenses. I wasn't that wonderful, but there were only about five blocks to go around in Clinton. The town was still running wild with Baptists and their happy morbid meetings. We had heard a rumor of five Catholics in town. Maybe twelve Episcopals too. Members of these churches made graven images and served them. Also they drank.

But I knew the lakes and the muddy creeks and some music and I had forgotten caring about religion one way or another.

There was a place where I could go with my own war. I would line up plastic soldiers against the door and shut it and then shoot my Daisy beebee gun against the door. The ricochets, coming right toward my face, were the enemy firing back. One of the beebees chipped my tooth and there was blood in my mouth. At that point I knew the enemy would fire back and I wanted no part of war anymore.

❑ ❑

When we were in our tuxedos and were playing in the Jackson Symphony Orchestra, riding over there in Wyatt Newman's old Jaguar sedan, we rode past the smart hedges around Murrah High School auditorium. We'd picked up a very tall gentle percussionist named Hugh. That was back in the main part of Jackson, on North State Street. We passed a ragged man selling papers. The newspapers in Jackson were right-wing racist documents. Even I knew it. Just as I know today that Mississippi College is owned by frowning fat Christians. The school has gone away. In my tuxedo, I lit up a Picayune and stared out at the man selling papers.

"Look at that poot peddling papers," I said.

There was a huge silence in the car.

When we let Hugh out at the back of the auditorium, Joe Brown said to me, "Do you realize that what you said about the 'poot peddling papers' is everything that Hugh is against? That kind of insensitivity is what keeps him so nervous."

I guess I was wrong and Brown was right. Hugh was so tall and had an Adam's apple like Ichabod

Crane. He was shaking all the time, too. But he played perfect kettledrums, never understated, never overstated. Brown was his understudy, I guess, sometimes doing a roll on a snare drum when the orchestra did an adventurous symphony. I was third chair and did about ten notes an hour. I was in my tuxedo but I was bored to a condition of glassiness.

I was such a factotum in the orchestra that they got me to go out and get some little lady's harp from her house and haul it in. Her name was Lina Kellum, I believe. Three of us would go to her house and haul out this enormous harp. Her husband was the flute player, first chair, and he was so much better than the rest of us that he was always angry. Somebody told me he was Jewish. He was the first Jewish guy I ever met. His wife Lina weighed about ninety and she had an enormous flowing gown on her. She was so grateful about our lifting the great harp into the station wagon and getting it to the auditorium that we ignored the trouble.

She was a fine harp player, although I thought the instrument was ridiculous.

Twenty years later I saw a woman in Venice, California, strumming a giant harp like Lina's near the ocean. She had on a gown too and she was sprawled out there straddling her instrument, with her record albums for sale. Behind me, on roller skates, was a mulatto in a turban playing Jimi Hendrix tunes with a pighead amp wrapped on him and an old Fender Stratocaster, playing it as he skated, turning back and forth on his wheels, self-charged, squatting and rising as he rolled along. A white rock-and-roll band was going just a hundred yards away. The guys were so ugly and white they looked like they'd been doing nothing but shooting heroin and living in a cave for two years. All of us wanted music.

I was there trying to write a good screenplay with music in it for Robert Altman. With all my striving, I had only grown to five feet nine inches' height. A giant black in a lavender latex outfit, white Stetson hat on his head, with a white cane to guide him on his skates, rolled up beside me. He had great muscles in his arms and his legs that you only get in a penitentiary.

"You're him, ain't you?" he demanded.

"Who?"

"Him, baby. You're him, ain't you?"

I wasn't drinking then and had a tan and he had mistaken me for the television star John Ritter. Then he looked at me through his sunglasses a while longer. When he saw I wasn't John Ritter the disgust began accumulating in his eyes.

"You ain't nobody," he said.

"Don't get angry," I begged him. He was getting enraged.

I've always avoided fights by ignoring the looming person in my face. I looked down the boardwalk at the mulatto man playing Jimi Hendrix as he squatted and rose and then twisted on his skates. It was the Olympics of the weird out here in California, and I was just a small boy from Mississippi, so broke I had no ride except the green Triumph motorcycle lent me by John Quisenberry, Annapolis graduate, heroic Phantom pilot in Vietnam. Under the great Dick Prenshaw we made beautiful music in the Clinton High band. Now Quiz was a newly married lawyer in L.A. Our common memory was "Eroica" and winning "superior" in the state band contest.

When I was working with the kind and brilliant Robert Altman in his wooden mansion by the sea, I was in a tower of Plexiglas with sea gulls flying around me and the Pacific rolling under the house like a white man's dream of peace. I had a typewriter and there was a Spanish maid who would bring me coffee. But it was too nice and I had to turn on the radio. Altman came up and asked me how could I work with the radio on that loud.

I needed the music, the tinny loud music, to remind me of all the trouble in the world. I missed my kids so much, I wanted to hear how other people hurt too. I could not accept paradise. I had to drag in the bad music and the cigarettes. I had to foul up the air and my ears. With no whiskey, what else was there to talk about? What about all my pitiful little songs and my tiny eloquence, back on trumpet in the Jackson Symphony Orchestra and in the Mississippi Lions All-State Band?

What if I was wrong and I was nothing, exactly nothing?

□ □

Neil, a tall skinny guy, and Krebs, a short little man with a big nose, squared off in the alley next to the Dutch Bar, 1959. Art Krebs left the bar telling us he's had it with Neil and wants to have it out. They came back in after about fifteen minutes—nobody messed up, no bruises. "What happened?" I asked Neil while Krebs was getting another beer.

"Krebs paid me five dollars not to hit him," said Neil.

Krebs retired as a major in the army about six years ago. Tommy Poates, the guy we burned up in the television box, is probably a full colonel in the air force by now. Quisenberry is a commander in the Navy Reserve Air Force. Only two out of our class have died, and they are both women. Ann Gill in an air crash with the Olympic wrestling team. Jenny O'Neill, Henry's wife, with heart disease in Houston, lying on the operating table.

□ □

"What if this *is* heaven?" I asked Horace Newcomb one night while we were riding around drinking beer. "What if all those who don't drink beer will never know heaven, and this is it?"

"That's a good idea," said Newcomb. "That's a very good idea."

What a feeling those first beers gave us, cruising in my parents' Bonneville, my brother's Plymouth Fury convertible, my brother's '57 Thunderbird. My family always had the best cars. The old man was so poor in the Depression he always wanted a good car.

One afternoon Gomar Wallace and I were fishing right next to the boat ramp at Elwood Ratliff's pond. We'd just come out to hang around the good country and have some fun if we could. We brought a couple of poles and some crickets. The big bream started hitting out at the end of the ramp. We kept hauling them in. They were really big bluegills and shellcrackers. We'd hit a bed of them. We had about forty when we went home. That was in the days when we'd clean them and my mother would cook them right up. Gomar's father died early. Then his brother was killed by a farmer on the wrong side of a four-lane highway—49—coming back from the Gulf Coast. Their family has had such bad luck, I cry.

NAMES IN PASSION

Krebs. I am not sentimental about departures. But I thought it would be interesting to report that Krebs shot his own leg before any of the rest of us were armed. That was when Quisenberry was throwing footballs through a swinging tire down in his pecan grove. He was lifting weights on the Joe Weider course. He lent me a puller to strengthen my arms.

The great villain in this piece was Hoyt Weems, who made everybody disgusted with themselves. He was the football coach. They've named a football field after him now in Clinton. Weems hated tiny guys like me. He was a tank sergeant, maybe, in World War Two. He was supposed to teach me science. Weems owes me about $50,000 for personal abuse. He received salary and taught me nothing except self-disgust. He was a raw, tough, ugly soldier, who wanted to talk about people burning up alive in tanks. Neither of my uncles in World War Two were like him. They were level creatures.

Krebs was with us at the Strong River. Wyatt had brought along his Argentine Mauser. Carl Lee had the bazooka. His father had just died and he was going wild for armaments. I had my double-barrel .410 and a .22 Mossberg with a scope, lent to me by John Kitchings. O'Neill had maybe a .22. Krebs had grenades. He was the only real veteran with us, since he'd shot himself in the leg.

The Strong River was a beauty with big rocks and white rushing water, pooling back up in deep holes where the streams ran in, like where we camped on a bluff with our beds dug out elaborately in the bank and tarpaulins over them. I think Newman had discovered the Strong on one of his travels. It was down in Simpson County, about forty miles south of Clinton. But it felt like the tropics. Horace Newcomb was there with us a couple of times. He carried no weapons. He was tall and gangly and very smart. His dad was a postman, a veteran of World War Two who had quit Camels and begun going to the Baptist church very seriously. I can't recall whether Joe Brown was out there on the camp or not. His stepfather was the head of the Mississippi National Guard. We had a wonderful stew going by the pool on the little white beach. You got the water boiling and dumped in meat, potatoes, carrots, onions, and at the last, sardines. George Patterson was there. His father owned the Army/Navy surplus store. You walked in there and smelled Cosmoline and treated tarpaulins.

Newman was out in the river with a piece of Ivory

soap floating near his palm. He was naked. New-man was a big fellow with a hairy bod and he was maybe the only one of us who was not ashamed of himself naked. The river was firm and green around him. I lined up the scope on the Mossberg and shot away the bar of Ivory just as he was reaching for it. It was a miracle shot. He raised his fist at me, pretending to be outraged, but the big smile broke out on his face. What a shame that none of the rest of them saw it. Later I took a quart of oleo into the tent to have my satisfaction with dream women. We had a trotline running under the bridge, baited with pork livers. The stars came out and were brilliant and heavy in the air. The stew was big and manly. We were sober and deeply sincere, although you had to tell lies to have any class around here. Newman was writing endless poems to some woman in Nashville. I had my dream lover in Natchez. My god, she was long-legged and brunette and nothing but little songs came out of her mouth. In church the preacher would be talking about Jehovah and heaven and the judged, etc., and I was out there in the balcony pew in my suit writing poems to my dream woman in my head.

❑ ❑

Just a few years ago, when I was a bachelor and very lonely, I went out to a private lake, snuck in, and had a line out in the water with a minnow on it, way down. I'd heard there was a thirty-pound catfish here. My life was over with Vera, a cellist at the university. I always knew we had nothing going, and she did too. I went to all her cello playing with the Memphis Symphony. She traveled around with me when I gave readings. I loved the cello, I loved her Porsche. Then I went out to west Texas and found out her people. They were just wealthy. My parents didn't know everything but at least they were courteous. I tried to teach Vera to fish and know the lakes but once she saw a moccasin swallow the bream we'd caught, she went out of her mind. Vera and her sister, a failed painter, had been spoiled so much they could only see a white room with other people paying for them to go to Switzerland and get another privileged view of the world. Vera was denied tenure at the university mainly because, as she said, she was "no good with people." I stood up for her, but I never knew the main issue was she was "no good with people."

I was sitting there fishing and nothing was biting, and it was very hot, extremely hot in July, when this young lad of about seven walked up to me and said: "There's a big snake on my pole." At that time I had a .25 automatic in my tackle kit. I had a silver automatic in my kit and I walked down the dam with the gun. The little boy was right. There was a snake coiled around his cane pole. Its head was in the water. What a hell of a snake it was. Back at Wyatt Newman's pond, when Newman was thinking Eastern and about to go into the Navy Band, he said: "You can't kill anything. They just regenerate!" I thought about this. It rose its head and I blew its head off. A lucky first shot.

The child said to me: "Are you with the army?"

"No."

"Are you with the police?"

"No."

"Who are you, mister?"

"I'm with the army of myself," I told him. "It's just you and me, son."

We sat there all the rest of the afternoon and eventually he got a good five-pound catfish.

I've missed my daughter Lee a long time now. Also my son Teddy. Lee used to ride on the back of my Harley, reading a book. She trusted her dad so much after we went out to Sardis Lake she was sitting there reading her book when I looked back. She knew I was a safe pilot on my big Harley. And I was. Nothing could happen to us on my Harley. The thing about the Harley is you know every tire rim, every movement on the wheel, every gauge: You're perfect.

I've missed my daughter Lee and son Ted a long time now. Lee was waiting late one afternoon on a dam at Elwood Ratliff's lake when all the rest had left. She was still holding her little pole with the cricket on the hook, nothing had been happening for the rest of us, but she believed in her father, me, and the mosquitoes were biting her all over, but she was hanging in. It was almost too dark to see. Something took her cork down. It pulled her little body and she pulled back. She waded into the water and pulled the long cane pole back. Then she had it and she knew she had it. She backed up on the bank. Same thing when Ted brought antlers from the woods, proud as if he'd won the Nobel Prize.

Lee, my daughter, landed it. It was a redgill. A shellcracker. The biggest bream I'd ever seen. When it was flopping there on the dam, she looked down and saw it between her feet. She did not want to eat it or even have it. She just wanted to look at it a while and let it go. Which we did.

❏ ❏

Old Mama Hannah, who had no money and no home, was living with our Uncle Wayne and Aunt Jeannie Alliston down at Bay St. Louis. I had famous times as a youth in Bay St. Louis. There were shrimp and crabs and flounders in the seawater. Mama Hannah had no house, no money, and she lived from home to home. That was in the days when the children took care of their parents. My old man had to drop out of Ole Miss to take care of his parents. He was a smart man but he had to go back and take care of his parents. He was rooming with Senator Eastland (in the future) and they already had their stationery written up together as future lawyers, but my old man had his dreams shattered and had to go back home to take care of his parents.

On the the sea wall they're just catching a few crabs. I'm there. I've always been there. The high wind is coming in, and there are white spouts in the bay. My grandmother hangs into a big flounder on her cane pole. She's got it and the flounder's got her. She starts calling *whoop whoop whoop! Whoop!* Then Mama Hannah has got the flounder on the sea wall, big lover of a meal, and my granny brought it in.

Mama Hannah talked about it for three years. She'd brought a big meal into the house. Late at night, when everybody else was asleep, they told me that Mama Hannah was dancing to a country band on the television. Her hair was beautifully white and long and she had spirited eyes. She wrapped the hair around her head in a close way with combs in it. When she was put in the grave I saw my old man with his beautiful white hair sitting by the graveside. It was over in Forest, Mississippi. All the rest of the relatives were there, but I only remember my father and his elegant white hair and his courtly bearing. That's where I came from, Scott County, in the middle of the state. Pines, oaks, ashes, going crazy with squirrels.

My uncle ran Roosevelt State Park. My word, how I loved to visit with Aunt Bertha and Uncle Slim and all their boys. I swam in the lake with Ted Hannah and caught bream and watched the speedboats going by. The Lodge was an exquisite place, with its dance floor and the juke box. The trees leaning in close to the lanes at twilight. The World War Two tank sitting there for us all to climb around and get in. The real business. The WPA or the CCC or somebody did the parks all over the states in the Depression. We had cabins and stone lodges, giving people work. My Aunt Bertha would cook us fried squirrels and slaw and potatoes. At night we had a Jeep to run around in. Off the diving platform Mrs. Something got parked and caught a six-pound bass, but my cousin Ted told me never to tell anybody else; this was a secret thing. There was a name I heard, maybe I was kin to it: Tadlock. We had cousins all over the county. At that time "Searchin' " was on the juke box and I saw a lot of older people dancing. It was done by the Coasters. Pretty soon after that, Elvis broke out. But what a lovely place Roosevelt State Park was to visit. All the Hannahs. Tommy and Ray and Robert Oliver and Ted.

❑ ❑

Quisenberry called for me to be a pallbearer at his father's funeral. What an honor that was. His father was World War One. I never knew the man that much. He was silent when we played around him. Later, John told me that he had a temper. They were afraid of crossing him or he would erupt. Mrs. Quisenberry, Bea, was the wit of the neighborhood. She invented Cowboy Salad. It was macaroni and cheese and we all would have hated it except Mrs. Bea called it Cowboy Salad. Down at the Quisenberrys' house we had also a butter-and-sugar sandwich. Aunt Rosa and Uncle Curry were still there then, moving slow and wise.

The Ratliffs took us down to Florida. We caught so many redfish and red snapper that we paid for the whole trip. Mr. Ratliff never said much, but he had a magic around him about fish. He is in his nineties now and a veteran of World War One. One day we were out at old Mr. Elwood's lake. There were a lot of fish caught but a lot of moccasins were there too. Uncle Elwood got out his rifle and got one of them running in the water. He knocked off its head. Forever after that I've knocked off their heads. The herons were landing and the little happy small airplanes were going above us in the blue air and light cumulus. Hey baby!

❑ ❑

My first wife worked hard for me and rushed me into marriage. She was an army brat who thought my parents were rich. She was a painter and a lover and a wife, but foremost she made sure we were married. She hated all my friends. She had the great talent for taking the heart out of any situation that gave me joy. She had no friends. Everything scared her.

But now she is better.

She has a new husband and she is proud at her school. When you can't live life, school is a great skill. Take that into a zone and into another zone. A lot of people sit back in life and have their overview. Compared to my underview, where I scout, under the bleachers, for what life has dropped.

When I was fifteen, I already thought about a great uncle whose name would be something like Yelverston. When I went down to the coast I would see the great uncles, with their important boats in the water. A dad cannot win against the great uncles. Can never win. Yelverston launches the craft and goes out laughing with his friends. It's a brown cedarwood boat with a white cabin, cruising the waves and the people laughing. Yelverston was in my dreams when I was there and he was so far away. When I finally met him at Syd and Harry's and his son had been killed, and he was sixty-two and I was forty-six, I thought, All right, uncle, tell me everything and I will be your nephew, learning in the new distance. We don't have that many years to go. Things are shortening up. One of us has got to be wise.

Then I was struck by one of those meditative states, with no action, that affects men and women.

I could not participate in reality anymore. Could not.

There is a day for everybody who ever practiced cruelty. The boomerang, if you throw it well, as I did yesterday, almost comes back into your palm.

Every good deed and every good word sails out into the hedges and over the grass and comes to sit in your front yard. Only the creeps forget a good deed. We are all so loaded up with what our good mothers did in the past that we walk through life like darlings.

LOST PILOTS

Uncle Bootsy was lost over the Amazon, piloting his big plane. He was just twenty-three when he died. My Uncle Cicero Eugene told me about him. Bootsy never smoked and was a strapping good-looker. He played football at Mississippi Southern and then married a beauty named Hazeline. He wrestled a bear to the ground when he was a teen-ager and the handler wouldn't let him try for the five dollars again. He was after Rommel and the Nazis in North Africa, and before he left he laughed and told my old man that the Germans didn't have a chance, what with all our planes and fly-boys and materiel. In fact he laughed about al-most everything, said Uncle Cicero Eugene and my dad. But then his plane went down in the jungles. I have told this story before, many times, but my mother's crying is what stays with me. When I was just a tiny guy my mother would break into tears about her baby brother Bootsy. He has been listed as missing since 1942. We always expected him to show up, laughing. Maybe smelling like smoke from his B-25, but definitely there. He had always been so lucky and handsome and good. When he was a little boy a window blew in during a storm. Big shards of glass covered him. He was still sleeping and did not suffer a single cut. The Delta winds were still whipping around over the cotton. The sisters and Gran King and Daddy King, the plantation manager, were standing there looking at a miracle. The storm left with the silence of a vacuum and a green sky overhead. It went back into Arkansas across the river and poured itself into Texas.

Daddy King was known for his fairness to blacks. What a fine old grandfather he was. He died in the same room where I was sleeping. He'd had a stroke and he'd been blind for several years. But he loved baseball and strawberry ice cream. He laughed a great deal and he had pretty white hair too, combed back. He had liver spots on his face, and he was the handsomest old man I ever saw, although that is said about many grandpops. He would reach out his noble speckled hand to me and want to feel the glove when I was going down to play baseball.

But he had that laugh, most of all. I suppose Bootsy had it too, because Cicero Eugene had it and Annis Lloyd had it (she was my aunt in Baton Rouge), and the laugh through the years is the only thing that saved me, even when I was in Bryce, state home for the nuts. Because of drinking and shooting. I had a nasty laugh then and I was a roaming drunk with weapons in my hand. I thought I was enormously sensitive and a hero but I was also scaring hell out of everybody I loved. That was in Alabama. It was not fun to be in the nuthouse for five days, with the tall loony black guy coming by stealing your clothes while you were trying to get some rest. He wore my shoes on his enormous feet, and they were hanging on his toes. Like Kesey says, those black orderlies will boss you around too. They've been waiting all their lives to get whitey in this position. It's a dirty horror. One little white guy told me he lived on cigarettes and Cokes for two months. He'd been in alcoholic dry-out wards sixteen times. I got a lawyer and got out. Still owe the lawyer three hundred. All my family wanted me to go to Atlanta to a dry-out clinic for impaired professionals. They were there, my brother Bobby. I gave him the finger when I walked out. I'd passed all the tests and I was *compos mentis*. All I needed was some bacon and eggs and a good night in bed with a woman. Forever after that I've asked Bobby to forgive me. He has. He and Grace have forgiven and forgiven me.

□ □

1988.

Went to the fellows' house behind me, went over to have a breather and some of Ollie's ribs. Ollie is a black guy about thirty-five who claims he was in Vietnam, handling the M-60 machine gun. Maybe it's true. But he is doing a swell job at the animal shelter, he and Maryl. Ollie cooks great ribs. I could smell them at one A.M. I walked over there to see Terry and Ollie and catch some ribs. About two A.M. the electricity went out of the neighborhood and we were back to the nineteenth century, with just a little fire going in the yard. Willie Morris came over. Hadn't seen him in five months. It was pitch black except for the fire. He'd been working on a novel on the Bogue Chitto River, near McComb in the south of the state.

We walked back to see my wife, who was sleeping. With the help of Willie's lighter we found her. When she came out to the fire she looked smacking with her blond hair all ruffled out and her eyes dazed. She was in her baby-blue gown with white figures around the throat. She had our flashlight and went back to the house to get our dogs Joseph and Missy. We wanted to give them some rib bones. The little black female puppy we call Missy was given us by Mr. Levi at the Jitney Jungle. It sat on the table and ate a rib bone so ravenously that Willie Morris broke into tears.

"Look at her. Look at her. Look how she wants to *live!*" he said over and over. She was crawling into his arms. She had not been weened when Mr. Levi found her. Her mother was probably killed. She had white feet and a look from her eyes like all the good dogs do: What's next, friend? "Look how she wants to live!" said Willie.

Willie, who had just given a hundred and forty to the animal shelter, wanted to give a hundred more. Willie Morris has an enormous heart made of pure gold, like the beautiful old sluts in the western tales. He told me I must write a story called "The Animal Shelter," about the immense cruelty to dogs by human beings. Since I was listening, I recalled some blacks putting a lit cigarette to a puppy's tummy. I recalled white county people shooting the forelegs off a dog when they were through hunting with it, leaving it out to hobble near the highway where some person might, just might, pick it up and call the Humane Society. Who in America can ever quit the Humane Society?

❑ ❑

The aforementioned dude Wayne who was working with the animal shelter for a while. I bought him a car for $500 and he was supposed to pay it back with his work. Has an eighth-grade education, alcoholism, a divorce, and lives with his mother at age twenty-four. He quit and told me he'd pay back the car. For two months I never heard. So I woke up Ollie and the wife and I called him so I could go down there to pick up the car because he told me if I wanted it I had to come get it. I couldn't understand his directions so I asked if somebody else in the house could talk to me. He hung up. We went out on Old Taylor Road and I stopped by a black woman's house to check on the directions. Then I called him again and since we were near his place he was a little more pleasant. Where they lived was down a long gravel road in a sixty-foot trailer. The car was a little Subaru about '75 vintage. I knocked on the trailer door. His mother told me Wayne was out back. The mobile home sat on grated earth. I'd only met Wayne once before and he sounded so angry over the phone now my wife had brought along the .45. I went in back of the trailer and there was Wayne. He's gained about fifteen pounds. He's about five three, one of the few people I could actually physically beat up. I told him he was looking good. Down in the back about fifty yards was a garden. He and this man with tattoos all over his arms, maybe his stepfather, were sharpening some tool. The car needed a jump start so Wayne came out and jumped it and after a few times it was ready to go and Ollie drove off with it. Wayne had taken the tag off the car and I had to pay him for that and the jumper cables. Wayne was a cheat, a scoundrel, a liar, but he was proud of it. I was watching the man with the tattoos more than Wayne. They finally got the title for the car out of the trailer after thirty minutes. I was watching for sudden movements from the tattooed man, but he was the sanest one there. Some obese child of ten or so wallowed up and watched us, spitting a lot. We must have been something to hate there in our little silver Chrysler LeBaron convertible, which I couldn't afford. I really wanted out of there but Wayne finally came out with the title. I wished him luck. He told me I was the one that was going to need luck. He said something about the nigger who took the car. That wasn't a nigger, I told him. That was a sergeant from Vietnam. Oh *excuse me!* he said.

I hadn't seen real scoundrelism close up for a long time.

It was tough to be a repo man. But all the while, I knew that Wayne's pride was at stake and the tattooed man, Lester, was keeping him calm. I remembered the garden down from the trailer. It was neatly arranged and just starting with some shoots. I believe Lester was trying to give me a hand.

That was Sunday morning.

❑ ❑

Another Sunday, 1988.

All this day I've worried about what to do with this third marriage. It is a cold day in April and my wife has never offered to lick me or serve me food. She is on the picket line of feminism. My god, I've hired Ollie to put the azaleas out. It looks like a bad spring to me. Many Confederates and Yankees have fought over this land. I've told about flying jets in Vietnam so long and so faithfully, I think I deserve a woman on her knees. Besides, she has wonderful blond hair. I will snap my fingers almost anywhere, and there she is, on her knees. But she's on the picket line now. I never took her to Shiloh. I never took her to Graceland. Yes, yes. There's so much I've not done for her yet.

She's off the picket line now. My great sullen manliness is controlling her and she has no self-esteem anymore, which is exactly the way I want it. I am a terrible man.

Her beauty almost slaughters me.

In fact, I move through life without a conscience. Years ago, Wyatt Newman, who played viola and lived out in the country, took care enough to make some peach wine out at his place. He was writing poetry to his woman in Nashville, playing the viola, and being harrier and more mature than the rest of us. He had the old Jaguar sedan in which we went over to the Jackson Symphony. One thing that Newman taught me early was that endless note-books of rhyming quartets don't necessarily mean anything. While Newman was making his wine on the sly, Horace Newcomb came out to the place. We had rigged up a blank .22 and Newman's hand full of ketchup. It happened in the kitchen. Newman started yelling at me really hysterically about some matter. I had the rifle already in my hand and said I'd heard this too long and wasn't going to take any more. Newman was really large and when he charged at me I lifted the rifle and shot him in the stomach. He grabbed his waist with the ketchup and staggered down. Newcomb was terribly alarmed. He couldn't believe it. Newman twisted all over the linoleum floor and blood was flying everywhere. Poor Horace had his mouth open and his hornrims went out on his nose. Newman would never quit dying. Finally we all laughed and it was over. What a relief to the brilliant and sensitive Horace. We went out and smelled the nectar of Newman's peach wine in the well house. It wouldn't really be ready for another two weeks, he told us. My word, how Newman loved the fine things. None of us had ever had a fine wine. None of us, in fact, had had *a* wine. When it was ready, right before the senior prom, I went out with Wyatt and hid the bottle under some leaves in the dam of Lake Garaway. It was near the road so all he had to do was drive the Jaguar right by it, step out, and lift it up. When I was at home I could get no rest. I couldn't stand it. So I drove out to the lake and pissed in Wyatt's wine. I knew he would want to go by the bottle for a trial before the prom, so I and Art Lee — who in his sorrow used to try to run over dogs on country roads — and maybe Krebs went out to make the test with Newman.

Newman took a big slug. He choked and spat out what he could, knowing immediately what had happened. He chased me all the way down the dam and I was laughing so helplessly in the moonlight I couldn't run anymore. He pounded me and pounded me until he was tired. But I loved it.

When I was in the first grade I got run over by a car and maybe that fouled my head, even though all I got out of the accident was a dislocated thumb. There was a hill next to our house that ran to the main highway. It was a brick street and you could look at the cars making their cautious turns into our narrow brick street. We would sit on an encyclopedia with a roller skate under it and race down the hill. We had great carts with big ball-bearing wheels on them, as in the Soapbox Derby. Cars were a great nuisance coming toward us. I liked to get a big auto tire and roll it down the hill toward the cars, hoping to cause a wreck. By the time the driver got out to complain, there would be no kids at all around. There would be quiet. But we hid where we could see. We hid under the houses, where only cats went, and looked through the grates.

I am looking at the television and seeing Navratilova and Lendl, from Czechoslovakia. Without their millions and the hired teams of dogs and friends, they could be dead for weeks and we wouldn't know it.

Look at the heroes lately.

Look at the heroes who are human and then you know what was there.

I have no conscience, I guess. After the hideous Sundays I've had in our godless clime with all these males on the pulpit screaming and taking, I must rescue our women. There's only one way to do it, ladies: make a big pot roast with onions, carrots, and potatoes in it and then get naked except for your high-heeled shoes, if you've got any legs and fanny left. He'll eat the roast and then sleep, dreaming about some bitch five counties away. You've done everything to please him but it's not enough. Good thing I finally get up and take care of the little woman, heh, heh.

My wife ripped off the tubes when she had pneumonia and came and got me, because she knew I was lonely and distressed. She came up to Syd and Harry's and said, Here I am. She was off the IV, and we made love and petted our dog Joseph, the Lhasa apso, a Tibetan temple dog, bred in Arkansas. He's just solid love and fur. He does not know how to fight. He gives the alarm when strangers are near the house. Apparently that's all the breed was ever good for. Susan is a beautiful, short, nicely breasted woman with hot gray eyes and pretty feet. She went back to the hospital at eleven P.M. She was covered with flowers and presents, but she still had pneumonia. The last time we got into a real fight she socked my fifty-dollar flight glasses into my eyes and busted them. I knocked her down and began kicking her, but then we called the law: our friend Ron Shapiro. Would you please come stop this? So Shapiro comes up and just listens and then it's all over.

What a drag. Now I've got to get all sensitive and write again.

The three of us — Susan, David Smith, and I — went down to see the bingo game. David had a tape of Chuck Berry on. The ride was merry, with all the green fields and the little homes stuck on top of the small fields where the little hills were. The Chuck Berry tape was going on, and I loved it.

I saw Chuck at the National Guard Armory in Jackson, Miss., 1959. He was singing such a nasty song and I was dancing with a girl. The lyrics were so filthy neither one of us would acknowledge them. Two days later he was arrested in Meridian for asking a white girl for a date. I continued on with my white sports coat and drove the Thunderbird lent to me by my brother. My date and I were so shy of each other we barely touched. Even a kiss was out of the question. God knows why she came with me. She was a poor girl named Sandra who lived on Clinton Boulevard. She had good looks and so did her big sister. They lived across the road from the nice cemetery with a lake in the middle of it. I snuck in a lot of ponds and fished but I never snuck in that one because of respect for the dead.

On Clinton Boulevard was another lake. I remember, always, the afternoon I took my first wife out to fish with me. She was angry and pale. She stood there and watched me fish for thirty minutes, then she said she'd had enough. She cursed nature and generally wore a frown. I was embarrassed by her, but we had a baby. I thought we could get together as husband and wife if she went fishing with me, but she didn't like the out-

46

doors. Her favorite sport was being indoors and being depressed on the couch. Now in 1988 I hope she's better.

At some air base in some desert, with no trees and the hot wind whipping by the houses, where there was barely a bush, somebody's mother got out a butcher's knife and wouldn't talk to the kids. She was silent for a week. She was nuts when her husband was gone. Worse, she became an intense Christian.

It is terrible to see a woman become religious. Jesus on the telephone, etc. Jesus sleeps with her. Jesus is asking her to *join* him. There is no record of Jesus making love with anybody. But he is the eternal lover and he died on the cross. Even worse was his friend Peter who got crucified upside down. Those were severe times, and the Iranians have proved in the last days how nasty it was. They send children against tanks. Moslems, baby, are ready for heaven. They die to be next to Mohammed. Mohammed on the phone, children. He's calling collect from somewhere in the sky. Only forty thousand can be there but he still calls collect.

The other day I tried to run through a hot Southern day, even in a Jeep with Rick Kelley. We were fishing, in a way. I had my old Confederate cap on, like Stonewall Jackson wore. He never imbibed or swore like I did, and I know why he slowed down in the Valley campaign, when the Confederates were almost triumphant and could have taken

McClellan and Washington, D.C. He was sunsick. He was just *sun*sick. I threw up and sat down in the hot sun when Rick Kelley and I were fishing, even just fishing in the shade. But I had had enough of asking idiots where the pond was, and when the pond was there I could barely see it for the old sick sun all around me.

MODERN

When I saw the Hollywood streets I was with my son, who was looking for a Les Paul guitar. We were traveling on the Triumph motorcycle. Finally found the guitar in a shop in San Pedro, where I was living. We were standing in a pawnshop and the fellow that owned it said no, no, he could not give us at the price we offered. This was a famous guitar. Po had just finished high school and I wanted him to have the Les Paul. So we quit the deal and mounted the motorcycle. But the guy came out in the street, almost crying, and said he would take the money I offered him for the guitar. We went away with it, Po holding the guitar on the back of the motorcycle. I have bought ten different guitars for my son, maybe, but this is the one I remember.

We drove back to Mississippi through the deserts and at the end of July, probably 120 degrees out there. When we got to Dallas and on to Shreveport,

I could smell the trees and it was the South, my beloved South. Home again. Back to Clinton, Miss. We were in my red van. For a while the gas wasn't working and we had to stop in Tucson, Arizona. A nice young guy there fixed it for about twenty dollars.

I love expert mechanics. These men with grease on their hands. When Ron Shapiro and I were going to Montana, there was a problem with the van. It was outside of Amarillo in Groom, Texas, where there was nothing to look at but the scrub plants and deserts and fences. This skinny guy rolled in after a kid had taken the front end of the van apart. The man in the car knew the problem. It was in the dashboard. He put the van back together and charged only twenty-five bucks. Let's hear it for the few good mechanics left in the world. Hurrah! Hurrah! Shapiro bought this huge plastic housefly to put in his restaurant.

We left Groom and went up to Aspen, Colorado. On the New Mexico border I had to take a leak and saw two rainbows in front of me on the prairie. There were the lonely rainbows and we got to witness them. Then we went five miles an hour over Independence Pass. And I mean five miles an hour, at night. I could hear the right front bearing going out on my wheel. It was almost done for, but God was watching out for us. He was tired but he was watching and it was, actually, fun.

When we got to Aspen and met the movie stars

and Hunter Thompson, I was pretty stupid. I'd been sober a long time and I thought that was the problem, so I, like a simple boy who had never had much of it, sought the cocaine. A bowl at least, from Mex Eller, who admired my work. Met Jack Nicholson and Michael Douglas, both delightful and civil people, but was too cranked to comprehend them. Forgive me.

□ □

Yelverston was a man before he was a man. He was early at everything. He was a good ballplayer but he was never too good. He was married to Ruth and then he looked over the territory. He went up in a plane with Ruth and they looked over the territory near Galveston, Texas. It was an old Cessna with no windows and you could hear the engine roaring, shaking the plane. Yelverston was just thirty, but he knew what he wanted. There was some vodka when they got back. She was pregnant and she wouldn't drink any of it.

May 13, Friday, 1988.

Just a minute. David Holman has died on the golf course. This date will always register in my mind. I heard it at Syd and Harry's from Bob Haws. David had the thick glasses and the mustache and the cheerful word. He'd had a heart attack before and he had lost a lot of weight on his trip to the Carolinas last summer. His wife JoElla and his baby son Jeff, two, lit up this little town and university. David was a fine teacher of Southern Literature. His father was the famous scholar from Chapel Hill, David's home. David wanted to cut his own path. So he did. He taught his classes beautifully and he knew good literature and music like the back of his hand. He was only thirty-seven when he died.

Today my son graduates from Ole Miss. His girl also graduates. We'll see the commencement and then my wife Susan and I will go to the funeral home to bid David's lovely body adieu. He used to sneak cigarettes from me, and we always talked about playing golf together. I was always going to get my old man's clubs and go out with him, even as the terrible golfer I was. He called five different people to play golf with him in the morning. But he went out by himself with his new clubs and died around eleven. They found him out there, alone, doing what he was bound to. Maybe he knew. Maybe he knew he was going to end up on the fairway, on the practice tee. Maybe he was playing for little Jeff his son, and for my son, Po, and for me, and for JoElla his wife — to go away with your sport shoes on, trying to get the ball to go into the sky and hit God's dumb foot.

The next day my son graduated from the university with a degree in journalism after an endless agonizing ceremony. I and my wife poured into the exits of the coliseum along with other irritated parents who wanted a smoke and a drink of water. For years we had been paying and hoping for this degree. We had been through the girlfriends and the boyfriends and the money and the worry. My daughter came with her mother. Lee was quite lovely in her high heels, her own high school graduation coming up in Tuscaloosa. She is now the "young lady," as all fond parents call their seventeen-year-old daughters. There is much to weep about in pal David Holman's death. There was the memorial at Waller Funeral Home, where his precious body lay in the casket, bound for Chapel Hill, North Carolina, the next day. That he will never see his son graduate. That we shall never hear his encouraging words again. Smiling, is what one of his students recalls. He always came to class smiling. My wife saw him at graduation last year, in the coliseum. "What are you doing here?" she asked him. "Just came to see my kids graduate," he said. He meant his students. The only thing he hated was mediocrity. That was the only thing I ever saw him angry about. Like good friend Ron Shapiro; you never heard a discouraging word from him.

❑ ❑

Think back, think back, and then come back to where it's always been, at the WPA lodge, the community center above the Hoka theater and restaurant on the hill near the water tower. When was the last time you played bingo? Bingo happens for the Humane Society. Sgt. Ashford, of the Water Valley V.F.W., in charge. The bingo board is up and the sound system is here courtesy of Stuart Cole, my neighbor, the refreshments provided by Ron Shapiro. Last time I played I was fourteen at a Catholic thing in Bay St. Louis, Mississippi, on the coast where the Catholics roam and put some spirit into the town. All the old boys from the V.F.W. have their brown World War Two hats on. Shapiro walks over and says to me: "Man, this is America, ain't it?" We cleared $130 for the dogs and cats. Everybody seemed to have a good time. The mayor, John Leslie, came, played a bit, and went back home. Leslie has been a fine mayor. He loves the animal cause too, he and his wife Elizabeth. "Everything is possible," says John. "Just wait a while, and everything is possible." He gave us a big building for the new shelter. Now all we need is money and good cages and good runs and air conditioning. Dr. Bob Guy and Dr. Harland contribute their time and energy at low fees. The town is giving, wants to help. We will get the great shelter.

❑ ❑

I have been drunk some and Willie Morris has been drunk some, but Willie gave $140 for the animals. Willie's heart has never been in doubt. He makes this little town swell with his dreams. Willie wishes the best for white black yellow and the animals, and his great soul lies over two o'clock A.M. as in that painting by Chagall with the face lying on the town. He does not have time to fix his teeth, he does not have a worrying wife like me, he does not have the carefully made house with its appointments and the toothbrushes and the vitamin tablets and the nooky. But he continues, like a truck of love, spilling love on the highway. Down to McComb in the beauty round the Bogue Chitto. Writing his novel. Getting the lines straight from the moon and the weeds near the river. The both of us have come back to this pretty and humane town to practice secular humanism as hard as we can. That is when we're just staring out of windows trying to see even the rough face of God in the clouds or in the vapor over the oil spots in the parking lot of the Jitney Jungle.

Yelverston was a man of sixty-two years. His son had gotten married after he'd finished Yale. The girl was perfect. They'd lived together for three years and then got married near the grape arbor of an old friend of Yelverston's in Ocean Springs. Yelverston was divorced but his wife was also there, with her new younger husband, and Yelverston liked the man, and felt aglow with a new appreciation of his old wife, who looked elegant and friendly in her yellow gown, with the trim ankles he'd always adored. Everybody was paid for and happy. It was sublime how his ex-wife smiled and said just the nice soft things to inquirers, never trying to bully the conversation. He went off into a rose garden and wept for his good fortune. He had three million and a half and he was very satisfied that he had no more envy, sorrow, or littleness in him. He was tan and had only a little stomach and he had no wife at all. The sun was coming over the low limbs of the live oak and through the Spanish moss and shot on ahead with an orange glow over the roses and azaleas. He looked backward to see his son and his bride, a slim girl with nice breasts in her wedding gown. Life could hardly be better. The girl even had a crush on *him* and he knew it. He looked back to the tables full of seafood and the black men in livery standing around them. You could live here for a month on the soft-shell crabs and the scallops themselves, he thought. You could live off the West Indies slaw falling out of the bowl. Plus the lobsters the little kids are slobbering over. Jimmy Buffett came up close to Yelverston and strolled around, in his red moccasins. "Didn't I buy you?" asked Buffett. "No," said Yelverston.

Yelverston met with an older friend of his son's who was a publisher for a North Carolina small press. They met at Primo's restaurant, in Jackson. Young Ben took Yelverston along with him to meet Mona Neary, the genius of American literature. It was at a house near some college. The young publisher Ben knocked on the door and then knocked again. There was no answer but they heard a rustling out back and walked back quietly to see the actual lady, Mona Neary, a legend of world literature, leaning over some tomato plants with some scissors. They moved along the fence silently and Ben was about to call out to her when she fell into the tomato plants and farted violently over and over. Not only was she a legend but she was a blameless legend of world literature and her sensitivity toward all humankind was deep and wise. She could write about an old darkie on a bicycle as if somebody gave a shit. Yelverston was embarrassed and so was Ben and they hustled back to the front door as if they had never been there. They waited around a while and then Yelverston got tired and fired up a Pall Mall. The old woman opened the front door and said: "Well. Welcome." She poured them great tea glasses full of bourbon and then went out to the kitchen a long time. Ben wanted her to do one of her old stories on Japanese paper, very special edition. It was about BeeBee and Juju getting married. They got married in the Delta, where everybody was especially stupid but deep. Ben and Yelverston waited for Mona Neary, and finally she came back, claiming she had a headache. She had been blameless and sensitive so long, and Yelverston felt for her. Ben told Yelverston when they got in the rented Cadillac that Mona was tough as nails and hated heterosexual male writers. Yelverston really didn't care that much anymore.

He was hoping he would not have to be bent over and mutilated by the burden of history when he got old. How awful, he thought, to be so smart and so old.

❏ ❏

Yelverston went to North Dakota for a conference and saw the B-52s at the SAC base. They took him down the tarmac and he looked in at the planes with crews on ready. They were earnest young men with short haircuts. They were younger than his son, most of them. With these great jet engines and these awful munitions. There were some older men with gray crewcuts who Yelverston presumed were pilots or hydrogen-bomb experts. There was a terribly short little man in a sweater and a colonel's badge on him. The man was only five feet tall. His hair was coal black and he was a colonel. He was explaining about security and what he couldn't show them. Yelverston was six feet three inches tall. There was this deep croaking voice beneath him. He could not even see the man's name tag. "At the ready moment, conditions . . ." What the hell was the little man saying? Then Yelverston went back with the executives to the Best Western motel, where there was a cheese and wine gathering near the indoor pool. Norman Mailer and Alex Haley were there, and they were right fellows, he was glad to meet them. Kelly Skampton was there. She wore cowboy boots but lived in Charlottesville and had big teeth. She dropped a French phrase and Yelverston moved away.

"I saw you at the base," a young woman said to him.

She was the wife of one of the air force pilots and she was well formed. It was a mixture of the literary conference and the circuit board people and the air force. The young woman was tall and the short colonel was really drunk but he came just to her nipples and started his deep voice. To Yelverston she looked like the hoyden, the cruel coy one of his youth around the desks of Meridian High School. He was striking up a Pall Mall when she backed away from the colonel and pushed her rear against his pants.

He went out with her to the miserable apartment where she lived. She was showing him photograph after photograph of B-52s in in the air. "What horrible boredom," Yelverston said.

They drove back to the motel where his clothes were all lying around the room like he was a slob.

"Don't be quick," she said.

He was slow but his heart wasn't there. There was a forty-eight-year-old woman, British, back at home in Connecticut who loved him and waited for him and could take him full up her bottom while she gasped more more more.

The next day the girl was gone and he was lying on the wild bed staring at the pair of high heels she'd left behind, when the phone rang and he found out his son was dead.

There was a pint of Jack Daniel's in his suitcase

and he found it and drank it down almost immediately. Then he went to the bathroom and threw up. His son had been murdered along the Tombigbee waterway by dope pirates who were running free. His son's wife had been wounded by a shotgun. She was in the Tupelo hospital. Most of her right hand was gone. Yelverston could not weep. He wanted to but he sat on the bed with his heart beating all the way up in his throat. For an hour he sat there, wanting to be dead. Then he picked up the phone and dialed it.

❑ ❑

Yelverston talked to the sheriff after the funeral. The sheriff had attended the funeral himself and Yelverston was touched. Here in Ocean Springs, where his son and his bride had danced radiant and gorgeous, they buried Yelverston's lad. He had expressed a desire to his wife that he never wanted to leave the Mississippi coast. This was her home, and he wanted it to be his too. So that was fine with Yelverston, who had lived in Pascagoula in the forties and dealt with the shipyards. Yelverston's wife was angry with him the fifteen years they lived together. Now at the funeral she resumed her anger and simply glared at him. Maybe it was his fault. He was a strong-willed man and maybe he had not taught his son enough about survival, too busy getting his own way. They had shot a few guns together, but only at beer cans and alligators. And they never tried to hit the snout or the eyes, just let him know they were there.

Yelverston was looking around for her young new husband but he couldn't find him. She kept glaring at him as he walked away and took his car back to the motel. The car was a beige Mercury Cougar without even a radio. He was ashamed of his money and his success and he wanted to be obscure. The words of the kind sheriff were in his mind and he lay back and took a long nap. He was so tired and so weak and so guilty he could not stand it anymore and he was released into a peaceful nap of no more than two hours, when he awoke to a light rapping on his door. He was in his shorts and he lifted himself and got his robe. His stomach had gotten a little large and he sucked it in. His eyes were wide and he was racing with a blessed peace when he opened the door.

It was his ex-wife: father, mother, son, morning when you watched your son with his little neck leaning out of his highchair and first ate his cereal. All of it except the frown and the hate was gone from her face and she had got so lean with dark circles under her eyes she finally looked human suddenly to Yelverston. She was ancient. She was lovely. There was a mist falling in back of her in the miserable hallway of the motel.

"Come in," he said.

"Well, darling, what are we going to do about this?" she said. She'd gone over to the bed next to his and sat down. She was almost too skinny now, and if his eyes blinked and he had a rotten attitude about her, she could be seen as a slut who needed a drink and some money. Going back in history he could see himself only as a man with big legs who had never stopped running from one task toward another. He had worked in California and had a woman who introduced him to marijuana in 1950 but he could not stop running. He hated the marijuana because it made him giggle for no reason. He was running, baby, off. He had big muscular legs and he didn't even smoke until he was thirty. At twenty-eight he had his first drink, a martini, in Washington, D.C. It was terrible but he drank it straight down and ever since he drank it he was in another zone. He was in a zone where the little stuff didn't touch him anymore. He was very friendly and never angry. He arranged bowling pins in his fireplace. He would shoot a beebee gun at them instead of bowling, and the beebees would bounce back at him and he would dodge them. Every time he shot at the bowling ball and the pins in his fireplace, with the fire roaring behind, something would come back to him. He was smiling once when a beebee hit his front tooth.

"Well?" she called from the bed. She was so haggard and though blonded looked nothing as good as his forty-eight-year-old British woman in Connecticut, whom he could barely recall now.

Yelverston was just in his robe and his shorts, with his gray hair splattered apart.

"Tell me what the sheriff told you," she said.
She wanted vengeance just like he did.

I finally met Yelverston one night at Syd and Harry's when the music was raging but he looked so sad and distinguished we went downstairs to talk.

The next day my wife and I went over to Tuscaloosa to see my daughter graduate from County High School. I'd made the trip a thousand times on 45 to 82 and had called my old friend Pat Hermann up to have dinner with us at the Red Lobster. He and Jeannie were having trouble with their daughter Sophie, who had run away to Nashville. We met at the Red Lobster with my handsome son Teddy, and my sweet faithful wife Susan, with her hair swept back and the big rose on her bosom and her black shirt and her black hose. Old Pat came in with his gray hair like mine.

In the symphony you announce men like Pat Hermann with a soft chorus of trumpets. He comes in with his Mexico sandals and what a great thing to see my old Chaucerian buddy. We'd eaten all the seafood in the place and I was stunned by all the langostinos. With the butter and the salad. Tuscaloosa is about five avenues with racing cars and the light rain coming down. There was a five-car pileup on the avenue just after we left. My son Teddy was once in a wreck at a light when somebody hit him. He had long hair and the cops did all they could to blame it on him. But they took his blood alcohol and he had nothing. He had an earring but he had no dope. Old Pat and I and Susan were talking and then we had to go to the commencement, to look at daughter Lee graduate in the Alabama coliseum. There was a lot to talk about but I remember only one big parent, younger than I was, black, with oiled curls coming down, and he had a chain on him with a gold emblem of the state of Texas on his chest, with further gold chains going down to his stomach. He had some kind of fancy boots too, baby. He was from afar and he was here to see somebody graduate. All I had was a brown suit with a smart tie. But let me take this moment to embrace all of Alabama. Just like my ultrabad state, Mississippi. We're all so fucking terrible, no wonder it took four years of hideous war to get Lee up there and give up his sword.

THE TIME

March, 1988.

Giving a party lunch for Jim Harrison and his wife Linda. Our publisher Seymour Lawrence and his companion Joan Williams pull in front of our shack in a white stretch limo with a black chauffeur, all the way from Memphis airport. Sam's got diabetes. Got to watch the sweets and the drinks.

He started getting thirsty. I was dressed above my range. I'd got a $35 tie and kerchief, but Sam in the stretch limo had already beaten me. Everybody in the neighborhood, including the black guys down at the ice plant, were stretching their necks out. The cars were all down the street for Jim Harrison but they had never seen a Cadillac this long in their lives and I hadn't either. Sam said how he never wanted a stretch limo.

I heard wonderful stories from Harrison. His little daughter was lovely and absorbed the town. His wife Linda was regal, dismissing my drunken overtures. Harrison wrote a note back saying we might all someday fish in a wooden rowboat and drink Diet Pepsi. He means take it quiet and be off the stuff. What a dream. I want it. What a lovely dream.

My wife Susan sent her son David to live with his father in Easley, South Carolina, where he would have all the advantages. It cut her heart. But it was a dream of David on the green and white team kicking the ball and having his beautiful girlfriends. As his father provided. David goes ahead as the golden son.

I remember when Bobby and Ralph were drafted into Korea. My mother was crying in the dining room as the tall boys stood in front of her. They were going down to Biloxi to fight again. It wasn't over. She'd lost her baby brother Bootsy in the last war and here were her sons going again. I was a tiny guy, as usual, holding back my horrible needs for the moment. I recall that Ralph, when we were building the house and I was getting in the way, got a great nail in his foot and went leaping and howling away to another room. I never knew much about Ralph except he was a good quiet guy, my foster brother. He became the millionaire in Texas and paid for my second honeymoon. We had the catamaran and saw the porpoises in Florida, and my mother went out with us and saw the porpoises.

My dad was there near the ocean. But there was something terribly wrong about my second marriage. I could never get it right. We had a big house and thousands to look at but I could not bear the big legacy of physicians and wives who never taught their kids any guts or sense. My second wife was a beautiful book-burner from Nebraska. She had enough of me and threw me out.

❏ ❏

Before us there were tribes of people wandering around deciding what to eat or fuck or own. Billions of people went across this planet, asking each other "Did you get any last night?" Then came religion and all the long-winded phony bastards like Plato. The guy that wrote Leviticus should be shot for boredom. Then came gunpowder and steel. The Europeans occurred with tea and gunpowder. Some of the afternoons were tedious and so they began killing thousands of each other to own shit. Then came Pearl Harbor. Then came America and Uncle Joe, who only killed seven million of his own people for, get this, an idea. Commie against Free. The preachers are still going at it. Jimmy Swaggart said on the television that he would sweep out a lonely mission with a broom for the rest of his life if that's what God called him to do. He liked to "make love" to a New Orleans prostitute while her little daughter watched. I dare the man to quit Baton Rouge and sweep out a lonely mission for the rest of his life. I dare him. If he will do that I'll fly down to where he is and play him some of those hellish tapes of his cousin Jerry Lee Lewis and help him sweep.

❏ ❏

All my nephews and nieces are a blessing to me endlessly. They have cheered me through the hopeless and stunned times. I owe thanks to my sister, Dot, and I owe much to my great giving ex-brother-in-law John Kitchings, who has been nothing but a prince to me. All of us together have been divorced twelve times and we are looking for the thirteenth wife. We are stumbling forward toward the great big bass pond of the mind, with gentleman Pappy sitting in the lawn chair looking for the seven-pound bass. Being both rude and deaf, so incredibly rude that the rest of us are just awed at looking at a type that could only have come from the Great Depression. Pappy is like the Confederate army. So awesome in his rudeness. Pappy is a 120 and still smokes. Cancer has attacked him but just given up. Pappy wants his children and grandchildren and great-grandchildren all around him, bringing him their hugs and their good news and their snapshots of even furthermore babies. He wants all the little children to swarm into his bosom and put their little hands in his hand with its speckled fingers. He eats a banana and has had his bacon and eggs for 120 years every morning. He picked up golf in his fifties and he had pretty tan legs, nailing the ball straight ahead and short, then putting pretty well. I saw him pitch one into the hole from about forty yards out one afternoon, on a green with a horrible left incline. He was so happy and his friends were so happy, I felt proud of the old dude and will remember the afternoon forever. In fact, I love my father into the deepest fathoms.

During Korea my brother played for the Choctaws of Mississippi College, number 86 on the football team. I saw him recover an aerial fumble and run fifty yards for a touchdown, into the zone with the crowd roaring in little Robinson Stadium. My brother was six feet two and I frankly don't recall that much about him since he was eleven years older except that he accidentally hit me in the chin with a swingblade when I was a toddler down in, what?—Pascagoula. The blood spurted and Mother howled and I've still got the scar on my chin. There were palm trees around and the wind hit them and made the branches clack together while the moon out on the sea did its best to light up Nazi U-boats and Japanese submarines.

Yelverston was a young man from Mobile then, very entrenched with Roosevelt's Democrats already. Yelverston had a mild heart attack when he was twenty as a basketball player and was disqualified from the war. When he first saw the destroyers under construction in Ingall's shipyard, his mind fastened on them as miracles. They went up so fast. He stood on the deck and felt the ship and its guns coming alive under him. He could feel in his body that there was nothing wrong with him. He looked out at the gray muddy channel. Within minutes, it seemed to him, there would be sailors and their captain, all armed, going into the war. He had a moment on one of the destroyers when all the noise and all the welders, painters, riveters went into his bloodstream and everybody's health was connected with his heart — the sun scalding the edges of the yard, and the gulls lowering and shivering in the outward breeze of the tide going back to the moon.

They were still looking for invasions by German and Jap when I was a toddler. Everybody was ready. After Pearl, anything might happen. The teenagers were ready with their .22s and shotguns. Blackouts were maintained and everybody was looking for a traitor, so I understand.

But when I went back down to visit Bay St. Louis in the fifties with my relatives the Allistons there was nothing but the bliss of the heavy cool salty nights. Big blue crabs in your net and fighting croakers on and speckled trout on your fishing rod. The freezer was full of shrimp and flounders. Oysters, big and meaty and succulent. Tomatoes huge as two fists and four deep green watermelons sitting on the floor under the television. By that time we just had to scare ourselves, with a horror show from New Orleans called *Lights Out!* We trembled, baby.

I had seen some spooky movies at the Hilltop Theater in Clinton, but these were coming into your own home. We had Dracula and Frankenstein and the Wolfman and something called *Children of Blood*, a C-minus wreck maybe today, but it was the first time that people of my own age were shown as evil and ate their parents. My girl cousin, Catherine, had fits of anguish during the horror shows, and we would calm her down. She was horribly afraid of lightning and thunder. She was a lovely blond woman when we were just kids. We'd hit the sheets, Woody and I, afraid in delicious safety. It was a marvelous thing to be close to Woody, Sut, Catherine, Uncle Wayne, and Aunt Jeannie.

It got hot sometimes at night and sometimes Woody and I slept on the porch, which ran around two sides of the house. Nobody had any money, nobody had any big dreams, nobody had an inkling of disaster.

On August 17th, 1969, the hurricane Camille hit Pass Christian and the southwest Mississippi coast with a force of 250 mph, the strongest storm ever registered on the North American continent. My Uncle Wayne was with the State Health Service and suffered a heart attack while working to relieve the victims. Water came all over the towns and corpses from graveyards hung in the trees.

Phil Beidler and I visited Uncle Wayne and Aunt Jeannie in 1978 and he was still talking about the hurricane. Uncle Wayne had had his thorax removed because of cancer and he just whispered to us. He liked the house cool and his watermelons, but once before when I'd been there and wanted to catch some fish, to catch up on our old times, Uncle got us a boat and we went out, but we didn't catch anything. He spoke with a whisper all the time and he was bald-headed, wearing glasses. Nobody ever had a better uncle than Uncle Wayne. In that brown water with his little boat and him in his flannel shirt. Nobody ever even had a better uncle.

DELTA IS THIRTY
MILES WEST

Ron Shapiro, with his white bent Oldsmobile convertible, has a home anywhere he goes. I have seen Ron fall asleep on a slab of concrete in New Mexico and Wyoming and Colorado. He keeps a log of good sayings with him. He's Jewish, from St. Louis. Was in the dry-cleaning or tux-rentals business up there, but his dad died early and I believe Ron is committed to having music and parties and now, like the rest of us, to making a living as long as the past doesn't take its toll. The past will cost you fifty dollars a day in worry if you let it, and Shapiro knows that only the day with your friends and neighbors really matters.

My wife and I were beating the hell out of each other one morning, as mentioned earlier, and the wife called Ron. I'd slapped her a few times and she'd brought out a baseball bat and we were both miserable. Earlier we had on love music and Susan had the house looking superb, even with our thir-

73

teen pets running in and out of the place. We have thousands of memories of our kids and the sanctity of our poor dwellings with our children close to us. Shapiro came right up and just understood. Did nothing but stand there with his long hippie hair and his bright black eyes and said, "I'm here, guys." I went down to the Hoka for a while and had a lunch of stir-fry and bacon. Then went ahead to my screwdrivers and my great tales of the war. I have a need to tell people about all the wars and Quisenberry's heroism. Very strange how I read antiwar poems when I was teaching at Clemson and pled with Quiz not to fight. Now Susan's got the Vietnam Memorial going at the university museums with the warriors coming in to speak of their experiences. Col. Flo Yoste is providing tapes of the air force doing its duty. Shapiro did his duty as a clerk-typist in Korea. He told me once that the girls over there were so available and easy that he could never really recondition himself to America. But when I talked with him at the Hoka, he smiled and said how lovely it would be to have a feisty woman like Susan who got out a baseball bat and knocked your fifty-dollar flight glasses into your eyes.

I seem to be talking about nothing but war and the threat of calamity.

The calamity is that we get only seventy-five years to know everything and that we knew more by our guts when we were young than we do

with all these books and years and children behind us.

I remember the great pride I had in being a pallbearer at Quisenberry's father's funeral. I had visited him at the nursing home. Quiz called me about
his father's death and I didn't have a working au-
tomobile. I had only my great Harley-Davidson and
I got on my flight suit, put my formal brown suit
in the bag, and drove down through a hell of a rain
to be a pallbearer. What an honor it was. I met
Jerry Lyons and Ed Ratliff and Billy Quisenberry
again, and we traded stories. The Lyons family
were always a sweet bunch of people. They lived
near the Dicklies, who were awful people. Peter
Dicklie and O. B. Leader were sociopathic scum,
especially when they got their cowardly little souls
together. They liked to beat up drunken people
and steal, along with Cal Richardson.

There was a girl named Marie Hoppe, the daughter of brass in the air force or something. She
wanted to get naked and use profanity. She had a
crush on me and told a friend of mine that if I
would just take her out once and respect her, she
would get naked and do everything on the next
date. She had no breasts, unlike Martha Barnett,
who was a flute player. And Liz Meeter, whose family is so violently right-wing religious in the Pres-
byterian church they don't give anybody a chance.
Liz was the biggest tease in high school and so stone

dumb you would see her going by the house in a station wagon with even more children, increasing the race as Abraham said.

Behind my house lived the Tighes, nephews of the most deceiving wretched governor that Mississippi ever had. My father roomed with Jim Eastland at Ole Miss. Eastland the seg millionaire, the power. I suppose when you give everybody a chance and a personal interview they all might have their charm, as Pappy said Eastland did. One of the others of Pappy's great friends was the president of Mississippi College, R. L. McLemore. Pappy and R. L. and their wives went to Russia together. They went through the straits of Finland, etc. My pappy tried to discuss real estate with gray-faced Russians who had no idea what he was talking about. R. L. and his wife were historians. He had a heart condition that finally took him and his wife was hit by a car not too long afterwards. He was a fine president and a scholar who appreciated world literature. We knew him as Doctor Mac.

What a sorry damned thing it is to see the preachers get in politics. They shame the church of Christ, which has always been a small body of believers who never even thought about having a Buick. Shapiro, the Jew, is much more the Christian than any of them. He brings love to the crowd and good food. Asks almost nothing for himself, until the bills are owed. He brings the architecture around himself, the architecture of good will and never a discouraging word, as in the song "Home on the Range." Shapiro is home on the range. Yeah, he is our native son, who can fall asleep even with cocaine in Aspen, Colorado, with Semmes Luckett and our friends out there.

They were filming at the Ole Miss motel when my wife and I went down and watched. I was stoned, I guess, from some anger over the missed plane ride, and insulted the director and the producer. But when I saw Treat Williams in a pink pirate's blouse doing some moves around the motel room with Ally Sheedy, I knew that this was really misinformed. A man wearing a pink pirate's blouse, after an Elvis concert in the fifties, would be stomped to death like a rabid dog. So this I told Treat. We went up and ate in the community center and by the way they have exquisite food on the movie lots. They are swell people. I've got a little money and some time now and so I think I'll just go write a stupid and misinformed story about all their hometowns. Costing nobody nothing. I *need* pickled pig's feet! I *need* to eat Updike's books and abuse Connecticut, Massachusetts, Vermont.

When I saw daughter Lee graduate from County High in Tuscaloosa, I and son Teddy and Pat Hermann tried to have a little party for her at the Best Western motel. I bought some chips and nuts and eighteen beers, but Teddy had only one and Lee was tired. She wanted me to see her Volkswagen Rabbit out in the parking lot. She was the smallest graduate in the class of 450. She was my last child and I always wanted a daughter. She is tiny and has missed her dad these many years. We will never recover the afternoon when we came back from Sardis Lake and she rode behind me on the Harley, leaning back and reading her novel. She used to sleep with me but then my mother and my wife told me that was not right, as she had breasts now and was a young lady.

I went through the lovely town of Olive, Miss., the other afternoon and thought of a certain reformed alcoholic doctor there. Get this. His daughter's report on him was that he was so smart he had to drink himself dumb to be a citizen of the community. What a loyal interpretation of the father!

We went through Columbus and I had to go into the Army/Navy surplus store. Columbus is where the air base is and I also wanted to go out and see some of the new air force jets take off. There was no deal there. They had security and I knew nobody on the base except Col. Edwards and that was late and thirdhand. But back to the Army/Navy surplus store. I bought a three-dollar shirt but I wanted the stuff they wouldn't sell. They had a snow-white German helmet from World War Two. They had a Spanish paratrooper's helmet, black leather with a gold heraldic device on the front. This was made so any spotlight would pick him out and the enemy could shoot him through the head when he landed. They also had a good boomerang on the counter and the price was only $2.98. After all these years, the price had gone up only a dollar. The better one was black and cost seven bucks. But I wasn't feeling very warlike then.

My wife and I had made some whoopie in the cruel old town of Tuscaloosa and we'd had a good breakfast with my kids and Pat Hermann at Wright's Bakery, where Lee gave me the news that she'd run out of gas last night and had to walk a mile, buy some milk, and empty it out so as to get gas from a hysterical Arabian at a late-night mart, and she got home at one. This is the U.S.A., night watchers. Arabs own the oil and they come over here wanting the other end of the pump. They also want white dumb wives, some of them. One of them came to Ole Miss and has killed both his American wives. They have pride and a certain attitude, you see. Several people have written long history books explaining how the Persians have a proud culture and it is all our fault. Shit.

Ayatollah rock and rolla. With a religious idea he sends thousands of children in front of tanks. The pope is a good number too. Goes down to Africa and tells them to multiply. This earth is not our real home. Die at nine months old with a swollen belly and flies all over you and that will prove it. Sally What's-her-name for the Christian Children's Fund arrived bloated in 1980 in her Mercedes with chauffeur with the doctor who was running the alcohol clinic in San Pedro. He was a meaningful guy, a smart man about alcohol and he helped me. But then Sally showed up to dance with the ex-drunks and she looked like a blond pig. She was eating enough for seven children herself. For just fifty cents a day you can feed one twentieth of me. And the whining voice. The voice that even makes you dismiss starving Peruvian children. Michael Jackson and the rest come in, "We Are the Children" etc. Michael says God wrote the lyrics. Like God replaced his original face with that of Diana Ross. But god knows we need our rich phony celebrities. Some food got to some mouths and that is the bottom line, eh?

DOGS

The dogs at the animal shelter have been infected with distemper. Twenty-seven of them had to go down two weeks ago. Now twenty new dogs have to go down. All the trouble and all the food and the care that Ollie and Maryl have been giving avails nought. All the creatures with their front feet lifted to you, man's best friend multiplied by forty, wanting you for their lifetime pal. Please, please.

There's a cruel old alcoholic fart down at the Gin named Pete who said he would pass by a crushed human being in the road but could not help but stop for a dog in need. He was talking through the vodka of course. He wouldn't stop for anything if it got in the way of his next drink. He wants to tell the story of his education and his girlfriend and the contacts he has. He says that his "moniker" is "Fast Pete," earned by his expertship on the pool table. He also mentioned that "Nosferatu" was simply German for *vampire*. He was trying to impress me and all the hungover slobs in the Gin. Mickey has been down there for centuries but he just gives the encouraging hand and never even mentions his poems, which are quite good. A stone wino, he doesn't try to impress anybody. Come on come on come on come on come on don't you know me I've always been there just your brilliant pal let me give you some advice all I know about the interworld situation have another yes let me pay for it must come up to my house where I can show all the pictures and all the culture and the music in my very private precious house have I told you the number of gooks I killed? Man, have I had wives. Have I had money? Have I known some stars? Can you understand Faulkner, I have to make a big effort. Sorry I vomited.

Almost all the news is in and the class of '60, Clinton High, has been an exceptional class. Despite Coach Hoyt and Emma Wills and Superintendent Milkness, we did get educated. Despite Coach Hooks and the enormous insensitivity of Billy Nick Farte and the enormous worthless Coach Nichols, many of us have lived lives of substance. Lois Blackwell was the one. And Mrs. King in Latin. And last, *sine qua non*, superlative, Dick Prenshaw. He and Mrs. Blackwell told us about a whole different world.

He and Barnett, the student assistant from the college. Barnett wore a blue suit and was always talking about sucking his wife's pussy. We saw Barnett's senior recital when he played a really difficult piece by Rafael Mendez that ended on a high E above high C. He did the whole thing brilliantly but it was one of those that depended on the last ultrahigh E. Barnett had his jaws out and hips ready but the E wouldn't come. He just sort of became a balloon around his trumpet, and nothing happened. It was total silence and all of us afriended of Barnett looked away into the shameful aisles. I was giggling but I am a low bastard anyway. I looked over to Barnett's good-looking wife and could not believe he had said that about her. She seemed so innocent but on the other hand you looked at her ankles and her impatient feet. I had never imagined love like that and I wanted to lasso with my tie her ankles in their black stockings. I would pull off both her stockings and set them on fire. By that time I had possessed five lovely women on campus but I had never even looked. None of them though had the long black eyelashes of Barnett's wife. All of them just waited with their legs. With my trumpet and the little jazz band there was no trouble in finding women. They wore madras blouses and brown Weejuns with no socks and tan legs. But I had never been a lover. Barnett wore a goatee. He looked like a beatnik, but he described his beard as a "womb broom." I was my full height but I was so tiny compared to all the real men. I wasn't filling out all through even if I had my way with college girls. One thing you made sure to do was go to Youth for Christ, where the crippled minister to youth, Chester Swor, gave his antisex sermons. I was with girls larger than I was and they would get hot while he talked about "an errant hand, a willing thigh." I was a man in his tie sitting next to them and they didn't consider me real sex. I know that now. But we went by the ice cream place and had sherbet on Monument Street or whatever it was, in sight of the state capitol building, and they (two of them) drew my hand under their skirts. I would look straight ahead and then I would look at the pretty flushed face. I was in control. I owned them. They were in a helpless state when my fingers reached down under. There was only one who was good. She was going with a fullback from Ole Miss but we made love again and again. Her name was Arlene. When she was through with me she threw me away like a rag doll. Sudden and no mercy. I was a nobody, except now I could play the trumpet fairly well and had a European lover. She was hot one day and cold the next.

All through high school and college I had only the horn and my aloofness from the others. I was a horrible snob and the poems I wrote were difficult. They got even more difficult after J. Edgar Simmons taught me.

I saw J. Edgar dying in the V.A. hospital in Jackson, 1980. He put his poor slip-in shoes on backward and I thought he was ready to go down and have a cup of coffee with me. The attendant came up and said no. He wasn't ready to go anywhere. He barely recognized me and he thought I was from Texas. El Paso, where he'd taught last. His poems were about drinking too much wine and seeing Osiris at the roller derby and he had projected this work called *Hamlet Jones*. He wanted me to write interstitial chapters for all his books. I knew J. Edgar was crazy in 1963 but they gave him a bad deal at Mississippi College. The fact is the college needed a crazy poet. His book of poems *Driving to Biloxi* was nominated for the National Book Award. I saw him in a shopping mall in Jackson not long before his internment in the V.A. hospital. He was big-bellied and angry-looking in an orange shirt. I almost stopped and said hello but he looked very angry. He was an incessant smoker, as I became later.

You ever notice how easy it is not to meet an intense man from your past? How easy not to stop and take his hand, this weird genius who has the nonsequential connections to the universe? I was terrible. I should have divorced my wife right then and there and joined forces with him in the ugly mall. His wife and his mother had just died and he needed me and I didn't know it.

We didn't spend enough time with any of our friends who are dead when they were alive, we never are good enough and we never can be the old declaration God Is Love. Some shaky old bastard comes out of the depot wanting a smoke or a quarter and you turn him down. Horace Newcomb's father was a mild man who was caught in the Battle of the Bulge in December '44. He must always be remembered, especially on Memorial Day which was yesterday. He had a café in Sardis, Miss. Suddenly he felt religion and gave up his Camels and joined the Baptist church. He was a postman in a suburb off Clinton Boulevard and his son and daughter were smart as whips. But Mr. Newcomb never forced religion on anybody and he was just a congenial man in the house. Like my old man. It's the middle-aged women who take it so awfully seriously. Sometimes I think the whole movement for the churches is carried on by aging women who have found out when their children are gone that they have absolutely nothing inside except their beautiful dead son Jesus.

We moved too fast and had no time with the real people, we tiny and fast people.

When we were guys in the high school band at Clinton, we had a director named Dick Prenshaw. He was a laughing guy with great wisdom in him and we became musicians under his care. He was the one who cut off the wire because the principal gave his messages during our rehearsal. You cannot realize what an awful thing it is to have a dumbo principal breaking in.

Brown and Newman and Newcomb and me and Quisenberry and Hammond and Spiro and Kay

Sumrall and Ralph Parks and Sidney Odom and Charles Harrison and Nancy Lumkin and Kaye and the other Nancy and Jeff and Tim. With Prenshaw, we all made straight "superiors" in the state band contest. Jerry Lynn Bullock. Yes her, and Martha Barnett, and I forget all the proud kids, wait: Art Lee. We all were proud and march on because of Doc Prenshaw. I played my guts out for him and made the Lions All-State Band. Prenshaw had the first Volkswagen in town. He was an adventurous sort. I went riding with him around town and he already knew how to do it. He would pass by the normal citizens in Clinton, Miss., and say: "Yes. Hello. Smiling at you. Kiss my ass."

He knew what. In Mississippi we had superb bands, but at that time the Horn Lake band was the worst in the state. Prenshaw would call a few of the little captains of the Clinton band in just to hear them. Prenshaw was a genius. He knew that if he and you heard the worst you would know how much better to be. We sat there and heard them in our proud red-black-and-white outfits. Horn Lake went against all sensitivities. They were out of tune and loud and out of time. The Forest, Miss., band came on, under Hal Polk. They were wonderful. Then we came on and I think we did "Eroica" and another two good ones. Rusty McIntire on baritone. It takes manhood and good feeling to be a musician. It takes constant stupidity to be a preacher or an athlete.

Nobody much died. Called it quits. Nobody died.

Talk about smart-asses. We had the corner on smart-assism and I for one had become vile and profane in my thoughts, along with Brown, Newman, Lee, several others. We were messing around with a reel-to-reel tape and decided to have our own show. A tape recording of reality was a new thing to me. I had only three classes the spring of 1960 and spent most of my time in the band room. Coach Smith saw me leaving through the window one morning during "home room," as they called the stupid fifty minutes you spent looking at maybe half a poem by Keats or a *Field & Stream*.

I had a sort of band going and we had all the equipment in the band room. I had learned a few licks on the drums and saw the advantages of being a drummer. There was a girl who wanted to be on stage very much and I and two others went around supporting her in these talent pageants by creating a barroom scene while she sang "Frankie and Johnny." Being the drummer, I could look at her legs and the black dress emphasizing her breasts, and her Hungarian looks. We had been boyfriend and girlfriend when she was in junior high. Her mother was a stage mother and a half, a big-bosomed woman who pushed and pushed her to be somebody, to be famous. I whopped on the back-beat of "Frankie and Johnny" and the bass and the piano went around following her really wretched voice, but what high heels and breasts and black hair. Her mother had made her a public whore with a flat voice at age sixteen. At this time I pitied her and kept up the drums and got the other fellows there. Even when I was a college freshman I came back, because she was nowhere and I knew it, but she loved me and her past was horrible. She used to wear scarves on her throat.

Doug Hutton once mentioned in the basketball gym, where he was a great star, that when I went with her "head to head your foot's in it, and toe to toe your head's in it." That meant I was a short fellow and Doug was envious. High school guys can be awfully cruel, especially when they're around their coaches. Doug scored fifty points when Clinton High won in the state basketball contest and now he is married to Mary Sue Broome. He was a genius on the floor for Clinton and then Mississippi State. He was maybe five eleven, but quick and brilliant on the court. He could turn backways and slam it in 1961. We've met since near the Baptist church in Clinton, where he was teaching a Sunday school class. He and I in our suits, and he describing me as the only really famous person he knows. We were all awful in high school. There was a locally rich real estate salesman, a twenty-three-year-old senior in high school. His sister would lie on a mattress in the Mississippi College gym and take eight or twelve guys on. She was fat and wore glasses but she didn't want to miss out on anything.

Across the street from where I lived they had a gathering of hoods. Later I understood they were talking about whether to kill me or not. Luckily they all got drunk and just stole the hubcaps off my dad's Pontiac Bonneville, 1959. They did it twice and then I loaded up the automatic twelve and waited in the dark of our garage. I waited until two A.M. and was very sleepy, so I lit up a Picayune. There was a screeching outside and a guy got out of the car, knocking over the garbage can. He was at the back of the great long Pontiac when I got there. I knew who he was and I let off two quick ones near his legs and then the other two right past both ears. The car started up and left him. He went out in the middle of the street, staggering around, begging me not to shoot him. He fell down and started whimpering and throwing up. He had a hell of a lot of beer in him. I put the muzzle on the back of his head. Ever since that night he has been almost totally deaf and has left me alone. Luckily it was New Year's Eve and when my dad asked me about the loud sound I said it was some jerks celebrating too late and too near the house, with cherry bombs.

We made a vile tape in the band room. All the instruments were around us and we met at night. We'd seen the wrestling on teevee and we combined it with everything we knew about Barnett Jones, who "sucked pussy," and on to the big fat beatnik Negro I had seen sitting on the rim of the fountain in Washington Square near N.Y.U. when I was in the Mississippi Lions All-State Band, who told me,

"You want some of this?" I asked him what it was and he said, "Mary Jane, young baby." So I had my first weed. He told me after I'd coughed a little bit: "You know, baby, I know I lead a basically non-existent life and I want to go home." "But I'm from nowhere," I told him. "I'm from Clinton, Mississippi." "That's my home. Just four miles south. I'm from Raymond. I've had enough. Would you please take me home?" I walked off from him. Later that night I heard him read his poems in the Gaslight Café on MacDougal Street: "Stamp out the purple worm. Stamp out the purple worm! Oh Tarzan and bananas, let me go back in the shack where my mother was and there was no jazz and no sunglasses!"

They had a wrestling match going on but a guy would get thrown off and the baritone horn would sound and you would hear some slurping noises. Then you would hear the crowd roar as if there were thousands there. "Just a little cunt juice," the wrestler said. Bass drum. "I never eat much but entire cows and a field of lettuce and cunt juice." The other wrestler is a slimmer guy who knows the "science" of wrestling. He is assisted by an electrical shot in the balls when he makes a bad move. The fat guy flies at him but he ducks and rams the man's head into the pole, causing a huge expulsion of cunt juice and turnip greens. The crowd goes wild. Come in three trombones in a Bach chorus for no reason. Then the fat guy awakes and starts slamming the man of science. But his pants fall off and he has a one-inch cock and thousands see. Etc. Man of science kicks him in his huge horselike balls and shame happens. The fat guy's mother and father are there, from Joplin, Missouri. They both come into the ring and stomp the head of their son while the man of science has his way with the mother and then the referee has his way.

The principal found the tape and made an announcement over the intercom: "This recording is so vile and vicious, I do not have the courage to tell the parents of the children." That was poor Mr. Barnes. He finally got so old he drove a car through an entire pedestrian block. Never touched the liquor or the cigarettes.

Mrs. Barnes was a good teacher and loved my son Teddy at the church party where my dear mother took him. Reminds me how good Mrs. Bunyard was in the third grade when she let me write my stories and draw all over my tablet. Mrs. Bunyard saved me and my imagination, as did Mrs. Lee, Mrs. Harrison, Mrs. Burroughs, Mrs. Crane. Looking back, it was the women who put up for me when everybody else was saying get ready to be a Real Guy and make a living by being the same old things we are.

My foster brother Ralph was an ROTC from Ole Miss. He was at Lockburn Air Base, Columbus, Ohio. In 1954 we had photos of the Russians moving from house to house. Crypto messages, friends. They briefed SAC men on their targets. Gary Powers and the U-2. Enough said?

Everett Dial was going into the war but Dr. Dial knew a senator or somebody and pulled strings. Dr. Dial hated Roosevelt, the Democrats, Negroes, smoking, drinking, but he loved the little children. He was a doctor in Greek and Granny Dial had these wonderful meals, always: chicken, vegetables from the garden. Dr. Dial hated anything that would stimulate a man but he drank Dr. Pepper, which was loaded with caffeine. And still is. The Dials are fine honorable people, especially Murphy and Jane in Atlanta. John Dial, who has given and given to me and my family, is the famous uterine cancer specialist from Jackson, Miss. Many young men go to the universities and come back with their orthodox religion shot apart, Dr. Dial told me. While Granny made the milkshakes for my little children. With all this time gone by, nothing matters except Granny's milkshakes and the sweet smile in Doc's eye as he saw my little children in his house.

When brother Ralph came back to Clinton he met Joe Albritton, who had dragged Homer Ainsworth back from Pork Chop Hill in Korea. Joe loved speed and stock cars. Brother Ralph was going to go in with him and race stock cars. But Joe Albritton got in a wreck at the entrance to the Cotton Bowl on old Highway 80 and got killed. He came all the way back from Korea and got slaughtered five miles from his home.

Nothing is ever as you have explained it. Everybody is better off and worse than you could know in your furthest dreams.

Brother Ralph went off to be a millionaire buyer in Richardson, Texas, and his wife Meridith and his boys took care of Pappy in Houston when he was having cancer therapy at Anderson Hospital.

THINKING

I'm staying in, thinking about my people. Everybody is better than I am. I've bought everything for peace. Susan and I have a new king-size bed. My life is bountiful. It is like the Garden of Eden with a woman who is so good-looking I took a Polaroid picture of her lying in a bed in Biloxi with her breasts showing and showed it to my close friends. Sharing her beauty, although I hate her often. She challenges the thing: the *thing*. The thing itself.

Old moon comes over the ocean, blessing the blacks and the Indians and the white people. It touches my wife Susan and me when she goes to the couch in the red silk camisole. She's on the brown velvet couch with her legs in my lap and I take off the pants with her little feet and toes around the original engine, har. A waltz was in order but I had no good clothes and we put on John Lennon's "Imagine" and sat back. All the animals in the house came around us, knowing that something was happening. When we were in Columbus, Miss., at the Army/Navy store, the new boomerang, black and fiber glass, cost $5.98 and I bought it. It's still here in the room with its wrapper. It looks awfully lethal. It almost throbs but I won't take it out of its wrapper. Until the right time, which will be in deep Florida on the beach where Sam Lawrence has invited us and we will find our way there to the tropics in our Chrysler LeBaron convertible, looking all over Florida like Newman, Rankin, Lee, and I when we were fifteen in the Chevy Belair.

We overdid it immediately when we were fifteen but on the way back when we were all sunburned to hell and tired of hot bright Florida, we stopped at a motel and I was looking at the ocean which I was tired of at that point. But some teenagers were running around and I saw this taller older person with his back turned take this really fast spiral of a football on the back of his head. The football was thrown viciously hard and he never knew it was coming. He fell over but he was not quite knocked out and he got up howling about the person who could have done that to him. I was lighting a Winston with my feet up on the parapet. I started laughing so hard I almost vomited. Then the guy went off moaning that his ear was hurt. They were from Ohio, two cars full of them, and their voices were so horrible in the evening I just had to laugh. I was burnt to a crisp and needing the air conditioning but Newman came upstairs and asked me: "Did you see that guy get hit with that spiral?" He was collapsing in laughter too.

At a high school party out in the country off Clinton Boulevard there was this older brother of Claudine who was going to entertain us. He put on an Indian blanket and played the ukelele. Even worse, he was a sincere Christer who wanted to sing "Kum Ba Yah"—an African song reported from the mission fields. There was a lot of watermelon around. He was still in the Indian blanket with the ukelele when he got in silhouette under a lawn light. Four of us threw at his head but only I hit him. The spray off his head was beautiful. Later in the night I had a date with a woman who was three inches taller than I was. I had a smart car, as usual, but she was a real "woman." She lived near the Clinton Country Club on the boulevard. She was three inches taller than I was and already looked like a flight stewardess. I tooled around the handsome midnight and drove close to a fence on the north side of the club with a ditch of willows nearby. I let the top down off the Plymouth Fury and lit up a Picayune. By then I had some fame as a trumpet man and poet. I was wearing a white sports coat with a limp rose on the lapel. She was holding this little orange corsage I'd given her. The blue clear night poured in.

"How about my sucking your pussy?" I asked her. In getting this date, we had perhaps exchanged twenty words.

She hit me so hard right in the face that my blue sunglasses flew off. I saw some stars.

"How come you look twenty-five when the rest of us look like kids?" I said to her, relighting a Picayune. She looked away at the moon. She took her own pack of Oasis cigarettes out.

Then she started crying. Oh my god.

"Here. Have a light," I said. I was feeling sorry for her although she'd broken the hearts of many football players. She just wouldn't put out, even though she looked already like a mother of three.

"Who do you think I am?" she asked me.

"I have no idea. Why'd you go out with me?"

"I had nothing better to do."

It was a wonderful night for love and maybe I could have been charming, but I said: "Get out and walk."

"I can't believe this."

Maybe it was a mile to her house. I left her in the road and went back to Claudine's party. It now strikes me that everybody who lived along Clinton Boulevard was desperate and unsettled. People died early and grew up early and pretended early and men sexually abused their daughters early. I was left in a house with a beautiful mother one afternoon, mother of one of my classmates. She came on to me, asking me to save her. I threw away my cigarette and fled in the Plymouth Fury. She'd told me she had an ulcer, her son had an ulcer, her husband had an ulcer. All she did was lie in the back yard and get a tan, using iodine and saltwater solution.

❏ ❏

Yelverston came through town looking different from the rest. There was a fury in him and he told me he'd lost a lot of weight lately. He had news from the sheriff in Tupelo now and from his friend the sheriff in Ocean Springs. He'd gone out to look at the Tennessee–Tombigbee waterway and it was nothing but a dull channel between sides of slate. He didn't know where to begin. But he had bought a speedboat loaded with food, water, and two cut-off automatic sixteen gauges. His wife was waiting out in the car. Or, he said, his ex-wife. I thought he was out of his gourd, though I'd read about his son's death in the newspaper weeks back. He was taking one Jack Daniels after another. I said, Well, what about a helicopter, and he told me: "Don't you know I've already thought about that?" But he put a hand on my shoulder and said, "Lad."

I was forty-six and was not a lad. I was a writer here at the school and he knew it. He wanted me to meet his wife down in the car. His ex-wife. She was out walking around the famous courthouse and reading the Faulkner quote on the plaque about how much the county courthouse meant. Yeah. It gives many lawyers employment. March on, legions of the violated and ripped-off. March on, lawyers and your money. Center of the squalid quid pro quo and random justice. His ex-wife, I forget her name, but she looked pretty good in her long black coat and black shoes underneath with a flash of silver buckle. Things in nature gather round, espying the architecture where the fences and the benches squat out with a dignity ungiven until this very moment, this last hope for justice in the wild driven land the cunt with a hot seed on fire etc. Women exchangeable like shells coming back and thrown off in the weeds from a howitzer lanyarded by three poor fuckers from Germany or the U.S.A. or does it matter — the exchangeable women like thrown-out vessels wherein used to place some cock, etc. — where the shit is the end of this sentence, Faulkner?

She was a handsome woman and I shook her hand and she was very happy to meet me.

"Good luck," I said.

Yelverston was some drunk but he kept calling me lad. He had a driven look. He got in the long yellow car and they went off. Then I saw the police come around and arrest Blanche, Ollie, Jamie, and Buck for bringing drinks outdoors. They just wanted to look and then they were nailed by the cops. The police get $136 for the city like this and they get to write something up on their miserable biographies.

I always smile at the cops around here and there are a few good ones. I even saw one in the bookstore once.

Yelverston's wife was *Ruth*, again. I've got to remember her name. She was a woman with class and you could see it in her walk. There is a certain life to a woman's step. I've seen that thing happen in women since I was fifteen. No matter what has happened or who has been with them, they have a certain lift in their step.

It is like watching a friend come in, like my son, who walks through the house with some step in his sneakers. He owns the earth and doesn't even know it.

The night perishes and the morning comes back with its dumb challenge like Bukowski with the red eyes, looking for a winner at Anita. When I was in San Pedro in 1980 I was clear of the stuff and did not dare try to contact Bukowski, even if he would meet me. I went down and heard a Mexican band in a bar, two trumpets and a bass guitar and seven other string instruments. My god did I want a tequila or at least a beer.

But my son came out and I was fine in the little apartment with a color teevee. We were getting around on Quisenberry's Triumph and we ate down at the 22nd Street dock in a white Mexican restaurant. Basil, the South African, went with us. He was riding his Kawasaki. Basil told me he was so sick with alcohol he couldn't even take down water and just threw up bile for a week when he tried to get off the stuff. But now we were eating everything on the bay.

What was the show we watched, me and my son? *Baretta*. Tony. *Tony*, Po and I would call out. Robert Blake had that cockatoo and his dad and we loved it. Quiz and his wife Kathy were very hospitable to us. We ate with them up in Westwood and in Venice, watching the sea and having our coffee. Elliot Lewitt was generous to us all. For a while we were roaming around Southern California, just having it. Money and the Pacific.

❑ ❑

Back in the fond smoky days of youth Yelverston was never a youth at all. He was dealing, he was selling in his neighborhood in Mobile. He and his girl pal made puppets and gave shows for which they charged a nickel. Most children had never heard about a bank account but Yelverston had and he owned one. He did not eat fish but he would go out fishing in the bay and then come back and sell speckled trout and mullet to his neighbors after smoking them on an oil-can grill in his back yard. Yelverston's father was like Elvis Presley's. He retired at thirty-five for vague reasons, the more solid one being that he didn't believe in work, not any longer. Yelverston went to bed smelling of smoked fish and yearning to help his father even more. He would think about his poor tired papa who had worked in the grocery store so long and had an arthritic back and sore feet. Though Yelverston saw him dance and go hunting for ducks when he wanted to. These things made Papa happy and all his diseases suddenly went away. Yelverston's uncle was a rich man who lived in Hattiesburg, Mississippi, and he would come in and chide Yelverston's father as he lay back in his rocking chair. He would leave two hundred-dollar bills behind him on the kitchen counter and everybody, especially Yelverston's mother, was embarrassed to pick them up. But they did. Yelverston was selling boats, big boats, when he was seventeen. He would buy a bad one and then fix it up and sell it for thrice what he'd paid.

❑ ❑

Yelverston was valedictorian of his class. His uncle bought him the suit he was standing in as he gave the address to his class for three minutes. He was a good-looking man of eighteen, with unruly brown hair that he could never comb correctly. He could not even find a natural part in his hair. His uncle and his mother, Ellen, were in the audience. The band had just played "Pomp and Circumstance" very well. There were a lot of good musicians in his high school and he had wished often that he could be among them.

Yelverston had made at least a dollar off of everybody in the class. The teachers and superintendent loved him. He had made almost straight A's. In science classes, when the teacher was absent, he had taken up the book and taught the class better than the teacher had. He could read very well. He knew math awfully well. He had ten and a half thousand in the bank that he never told his rich uncle about. He was paying the last mortgage note on his parents' house. He could not recall what he said when he was valedictorian. It was something about poverty was your own fault and you should fix up your own house. Something about never asking for anything, never begging. Some message against cigarettes and how idle they were. The band cut in and he was swept away by his swarming friends. He had treated them all right when he was making money from them. The principal of the school owed him $500 for a boat. The daughter of the mayor owed him $2000. He got his diploma and marched out with the rest of the kids, only he was not a kid and he knew it. He went forward in his gown.

Yelverston moved and moved and made money. He never met a woman who slowed him down until he was in Arlington, Va. They needed him at the Roosevelt administration then and he had had a heart attack. He was only twenty but he had a heart attack. He was selling the port to the senator. It was such an amazing deal that would make him rich forever and while he was enjoying it he had a heart attack. Now he was even richer than his uncle, and his parents would have a respectable home. Poor papa with his disease, and his mother, Ellen, who had to live with his father, who was now, Yelverston realized, a lazy bastard with a foul temper. His father's first name was Larles. What kind of name was that? Yelverston realized his own first name suddenly when he was twenty. It was Barton. Barton Benton Yelverston.

A number of years went past and he was even richer and had a wife. For a while they couldn't conceive and then they asked a doctor's advice about it. His wife had to turn backwards to him so he could get the sperm all in her. Haunted moments when they had no music because neither of them had ever heard much music. They ground away in slow silence, thinking they were alone, in the dark. Then they had a son who once he was walking went and fed himself directly. He went ahead and did it. They watched him. He had his own little imperial strength.

The little man went ahead and did his business. Things would occur to him that nobody had ever mentioned and he would act on them. He moved along and he had his little schemes. He went through the day with his own agenda, as Yelverston said. He was always a strange boy and not especially beautiful, but he had a deliberate motion and he cared not for his toys and all the extra candy and silver spoons that Ellen brought him. He didn't want the big house especially and went fishing with little black boys when he was eight. He made himself a special fish bait, which was a roach covered with glue, hardened, and he trolled it through the bayou with great results, and he didn't have to change baits much. He just trolled it along with his long cane pole and he brought home seven or ten big bluegills and then cleaned them himself. He would take hours cleaning them. Ruth finally recognized that he was studying the anatomy of the fish. He was using a magnifying glass and working under a bright light in the utility room off the garage. He had found a *scalpel* from somewhere. He and one of the little colored boys, who was also interested in anatomy. Yelverston began eating fish when his little son caught them. He suddenly found them delicious. The little boy brought the flesh in supremely clean and Ruth would throw them into the hot oil with cornmeal on them, onions sizzling around them. With some lemon and ketchup, they were very tasty. Also when the little one was asleep Yelverston and Ruth would have nightlong enormous affections for each other, running into dawn, where they were thinking of the beauty of anatomy and the holiness of man and woman.

OXFORD

June '88.

Had coffee with JoElla Holman, the widow of David who died on the golf course. He's also left behind his little son Jeff. She told me she was going to go back to Chapel Hill, where David's buried and she has people, but she didn't feel like moving from their little house because of feeling for David and what they had here together. She was tidying up all the loose ends of the business. Little Jeff knew his father was not coming back and he was becoming anxious. David used to come into Square Books with Jeff on his stomach in one of those slings. What a proud father he was. His pride will continue into little Jeff. JoElla has a wonderful dignity to her. David loved her to the bone. He talked and talked about his amazing wife JoElla. He never had too much whiskey and just occasionally borrowed a cigarette from me, so as to feel like a regular guy. He loved good lit so much, he laughed when something was wonderful. He was sailing with the natural high of being himself and distinguished. His father was Hugh Holman, who wrote the handbook for the literary terms and was the great scholar at Chapel Hill. David was cutting his own track as a thinker and a young father. Every day, he would go to JoElla and ask her: "Do you feel loved?" He would give her a big hug. He did the same for me, as his friend. Do you feel loved, Barry? He always had a smile and the encouraging word. He adored Susan too. Do you feel loved today? With his thick glasses and his smile. He still comes into Square Books, a ghost with brilliance coming off of him now that he is merely dead. Since David has died I take nobody's life for granted. Everybody has a shine coming off them. Most are doing their best but not all of them. Some of them are still landed in the altitudes where they think that passing a dollar and keeping the status quo is a nice thing. Pres. Reagan has made a lot of shits like that feel comfortable. I'm not that political, but when so many criminals show up at once and want my dollar, I get angry.

The hideous man who stabbed the other 128 times in a trailer. There was a fight over a woman. Drugs were involved. He stabbed the other so much he fell apart. When he was out on bail he got behind some old guy at a stoplight. When the old guy was stalling in front of him, he dragged the old guy out and beat him up. Bobby Marks represented the killer. Marks is a good-looking lawyer making a living, has a fast smile, and like most lawyers who get their fee doesn't give a headache about whom he is setting loose on the streets. As long as it's the law. As the law requires. I would like to watch some of these lawyers react when the scum they have released collects around their back yard and starts looking at their baby daughters. I was down at Ireland's bar listening to my son on guitar. The murderer's father got up and danced like a low weird Greek back and forth in front of the band. Really, he was a joy. He was light on his feet and he was gliding back and forth like a balloon. He was dancing away from his son the murderer.

Buck and Dees were fishing in one of the creeks off Sardis Reservoir one afternoon. They were calmly fishing and then they looked up on the bluff and this fellow was yelling. He had on a full camouflage outfit and he was wanting them to see his minnows. He kept calling to them. No white man calls for another white man to come look at his minnows. Buck went up and looked at the minnows but he knew something was wrong. The man was on drugs of a serious nature or he was insane. The facts prove out that he was serious on drugs, but just marijuana. He had seen *Rambo* as he said later, and he and another loser went on College Hill Road within two weeks. He broke into a man's house and stole a high-powered rifle, perhaps a .278 — what the hell does it matter? — and came out on the road and shot into a car, killing a four-year-old child, right through the windshield. No doubt he had been deranged for a long while and when Buddy East and the police caught him and his buddy on some muddy motorcycle, he explained he was going back to town for more dope. He'd seen *Rambo* and he just wanted to shoot somebody.

I was reading Hunter Thompson's new book, *Generation of Swine*. There was some old Jeep in a pasture with plastic explosives in it. Hunter is a mature fifty, I think. Yet grown men were shooting at the Jeep to see it explode. Things get slow. Rick Kelley and I went out and shot four snakes in Jerry Hoar's pond the other midday because things were slow. We were letting off the twenty gauge at all squirming things. But nobody ever thought about blasting into a car with a family in it. This killing was so random and heinous it made Oxford cry. *Where do these people come from?*

□ □

At Eagle Lake in an old drainage from the great Mississippi River, out from Vicksburg where all the Union and Rebs had died for our sins already and now we were free to be boys and start again, we were in the trailer of Mr. Krebs. We'd bought some wine in Vicksburg and even Jerry Rankin, the future missionary, was there. It was me, Newman, Krebs, and Henry O'Neill and Art Lee, I think. At the end of the pier next to the boathouse and bait, with all those scrumptious snacks, we met Mr. Krebs. He was loaded on beer and smiling to have all of us lads over here at his humble resort. Thinking back, he couldn't have been much older than I am now. I really don't know why all the nice guys have to be so loaded, like my Uncle Troy. He was loaded but he made millions which all these widows suck around. I personally intend to leave nothing and let them quarrel about how thoughtless I was. We went into the trailer and got assorted and then went out on the lake with some lanterns and motored into a cove that was supposed to be haunted. Who was it? Krebs, Rankin, and me. We were sharing one bottle of wine, except Rankin, who was bound to be pure for the Lord, etc. That was all right. We had the minnows and we let them down. Big white perch got on the lines immediately. Maybe because Jerry Rankin had blessed us. Big things of two and almost three pounds were on the line so fast we were out of bait in forty-five minutes. The boat was heavy with fish and then my lantern shut down, cut off, for no reason. We just had the one tiny light to back up to the main lake and find our way home. The motor cut down as if somebody had turned it into a home mixer.

Eagle Lake is an immense lake at night with only a putting old Johnson, five hp, and a low beam. The moon was out and it had a beam right back to our dock, but we were afraid. Nobody else was around and when we backed out of the creek there was a loud laughing sound, a male's voice, off to the left. We usually had weapons but this time we'd just gone fishing and this voice scared me. They said there were a lot of dead Indians around here. A bobwhite went off next to the boat. A bobwhite is just a quail but this time I heard its voice amplified. It went through me and us like a shock. This bird was calling *darling darling!* Starts with a low C and then shrills out two octaves above.

We got back to the trailer and dressed the fish and put them in the fridge. Mr. Krebs's trailer was a great resort. It was capacious and we could wander back and forth. I got a shower and looked out the window while I was naked with the water still on me. In the moonlight I saw two baby armadillos play with their mother around the trunk of a tree. I had never seen an armadillo before. I thought they were Texas animals. But they were coming back here. The mother was feigning some little strokes and the babies were running up and colliding with her and rolling back, on their shells. She was teaching them how to be armadillos, bless her heart. They keep coming and they're so dumb they get run over by cars, but what the devil were they ever supposed to know about cars? Jayne Mansfield got killed on a road full of armadillos and she was human and once I saw her breasts in person at Gus Stevens's when I was young.

Brings up the issue of Camille Hykes. Smart as

next Tuesday, beautiful, so Sam Lawrence tells me, and now living with a painter. All these brilliant women live with painters. Painters are even more terrible than I am, and much more sissy. Even more conscienceless. They need like an acre of space, pretend to work for nine years, and then blame the world if they don't sell. They have a stoned vision where they walk through pussy and oyster shells with bare feet and never acknowledge what even was there. I have a friend who is a great painter and he still has no idea who he even married or what his kids are like. I saw one of his kids wandering around naked in Vicksburg with a dumb hungry look on his face. Do you know who your father is? I asked him. Your father is a great artist, I reminded him. The cops drove up. They were about to arrest him just for looking like a foaming idiot. I intervened. See here, I'm Hannah, the such and such, etc.

Camille and Jayne Mansfield. What wonders they are.

□ □

What a hot number the old girl was before she was considered for the Nobel Prize. She was old, really old, but there was still some juice there. She'd pour me out a stiff drink and throw her cameras at me. It was deep and narrow, I tell you. We had libraries and weeks named for us. If I could just take you over there, I asked her, and she said yes, yes, her mouth full of my kisses. Capote when he was really drunk called me the maddest writer in the U.S.A. and I was continuing on this reputation. For writers you can never give enough praise. We are solid babies who have missed something and we want it written out in big magazines.

Over in the Old Chapel, we hoisted the last of the vodka and I kicked her down the aisle. Die, die! I shouted. But I had to drive her back home and cover her up and kiss her forehead, having sobered up, knowing she was a national treasure. Went by to see Brown, who has a Jaguar and we both need it every day. Brown the genius from high school and college. He was the only one who could talk to me *de mano a mano*. Brown had the courage of his beliefs but more, he was using the brain God gave him and the rest of us were sitting by saying, Yeah, what a brain but would you like to be given that weirdness? It occurs to me that at forty-six I want all the weirdness and the fellowship of pal Joe's brain.

Pal Joe quit the booze five or six years ago. He was into it like I was and he needed help and he called me. I was honored to give him my professional advice from California, Montana, though since I've been a failure by AA standards. Brown, Brown, how we used to argue over some passage in a radio song, whether it was a violin or a synthesizer. That was when electronic music was moving in and I knew it. I was right. But Brown was never attuned to the radio. His head was in the great symphonies and the Bach movements that sometimes go into a sort of calculus and Mozart when he moves into the clouds with his smart-assness challenging a god to strike him down he has gotten so impertinent.

Brown, in room 421 in Ratliff Dorm at Mississippi College, where we were talking about Freud and Marx and the room was crammed with all of Brown's books and sculptures, the metal stork, and the neighborhood of the room became zero when they threw in this zealot named Tom Rawlings who edited the school newspaper, in a room about fifteen by fifteen. We had a stereo and jazz and classics. Nobody had a chance to live. We were doomed at Mississippi College. We had an atheists' convention. We dreamed about opening up the roof and having ack-ack fire. Instruments all over the room. The Russians would never get us. We were not afraid. Rawlings wanted to fight with boxing gloves and show me what a real man was and I whipped his ass out in the hall, bloodied his nose. Don't mess with me, Christers. Gene Speed came in, busted from the Air Force Academy. Then there were complaints from the dorm counselor. Joe and I were doing the chloroform just to blank out. The teachers were almost uniformly wretched. We had a small civilization going before. Joe's parents came and dragged him out. Then my father came and dragged me out. I will never forgive my parents for not allowing me my life at college, never sticking up for me. They were spineless, discreet. I got home and then married to get away from home. Who needed all the lectures?

□ □

Somewhere over the dying, '88.

Gene Speed is a doctor now. His father was a preacher from Meridian. Speed fell in love with Kell Gray and then wandered around her yard with a machete until Kell's mother let him in to have a drink of water. Kell was the drum majorette of the Provine High Band. She had a bikini very early. She apparently would let some men have some and then cut them off. Newcomb fell for her. Newman was into it. Older men like Charles Last came by to ply her charms. Speed was head over heels. I never cared for her personally because she was pale and had moles on her but other men found her fascinating. Speed was in 421 and was an atheist. I wasn't an atheist but I smoked and hated Jesus people. Jesus people were everywhere and loud.

But I was smoking my cigarette one day when a Christer came by and asked me, "Why do writers always smoke?" Speed was lighting one up near me and he said, "Why don't you run home and get yourself raped?" Speed was harsh. He fell head over heels in love with a girl named Eleanor and then when that didn't work out, he shot himself in the belly with a .22. Nicely. I was used to him because I'd knocked him out once when we were wrestling. He overweighed me by forty pounds but I slammed him down and he passed out. Speed was always wanting to pass out or be wounded. He loved me, though.

Give the guy a break. His father was a preacher who smiled at an organist or something. And got fired and discredited. It's happened. A preacher smiles and has the spirit and then a woman goes crazy. The preacher is a lousy man.

We're all all right. Speed, Brown, me.

□ □

We had some dates at Millsaps, the smart school. Speed had his date and we were waiting in a sorority hall, with the Plymouth Fury convertible — white, blue leather seats — trembling outside. My date didn't show. We were waiting, maybe it could be my wife, I was all excited. Speed's date was two inches taller than I was and a great beauty. Speed was about six-one and his date was looking at him. Speed was a fine-looking man with a smart beak of a nose and big gray eyes in a ruddy skin. He was erect too, and he had told me about my posture and my diet. I thought I was pretty handsome, especially with my rich brother's Fury outside. Finally Speed's date, who was so good I wanted to lick her ankles, confessed that my date had gone off with another guy, a football player from Tulane. Speed told her to go to hell. He wasn't going to stand for his pal getting stood up. He let go of this wonderful girl and we walked back to the car, alone. She came out to tell him something. Go to hell, he said. My god, Speed was loyal. He actually loved me.

When Yelverston and I were talking he was plenty drunk but then he sobered up suddenly with a brandy and coffee. He and his wife came up to our house, with all my books and the horns and Bach on the stereo.

His wife Ruth sat on the bed and talked to Susan.

I wanted to take Yelverston out to the Grove at the Ole Miss campus and throw the boomerang. I had the new fiber-glass model, still in its plastic. But when I got to the Grove I was changed and I just listened to him and never got out of the car.

❑ ❑

Back in the trailer at Eagle Lake nobody was smoking yet, the air was clear, and we had all these fish to clean. It was a miracle. Even the armadillos have children.

EVERY DAY

The birds are here in the morning and the dawn is coming into our lovely town. I've pledged to keep away from hostility with my wife. Sometimes propinquity is the thing. Marriage is a long-scale idea and you just can't live that close without having a fight.

I'm looking straight ahead to pussy and shelter and thirteen dollars. With that and a pencil, I can rule the world. The little sycophantesses in their tennis shoes will run and get the paper. I require the eight-dollar stuff at Square Books, heavy bond with ecru color. My god, all the pets are waking up and need food. We've got about eight cats and two dogs here. But that's all right. We'll move the rug out and have it cleaned and deodorized. Human babies get out of the womb looking shifty already. You ever notice that? Animals come out looking lively and ready for life. Maybe a case for original sin. I don't know.

What do I know, with my history of flying and cunning? All my seven wives wailing about my mistreatment.

I looked in the mirror and I saw that Susan really tagged me around the neck during our last battle. But I was a wild man and she was fighting for her life. She tried to kick the manhood but it was to no avail. I began strangling her and screaming out the ending of Poe's "Masque of the Red Death." I never knew I had memorized it. But then I left off her throat, and the vision, pure as a rhapsody from the weirs, trembled and yet stood her poise, against the green curtains and the smoke.

Top off the convertible and we're doing just twenty in an old forgotten place where the poplars are hanging over and we go into a tunnel of sudden shade, lost to the world, no horns no sirens no red light. Both of us hungry for a bite and only a half a Pepsi left. Out of cigarettes, no stimulants at all. At the end of the tunnel is a decayed barn, faded red and very picturesque. Just for the hell of it and for old Walt Whitman and Mark Twain and the boys who said themselves so well, I burn up a five-dollar bill while she sucks my person. This is the sort of squalor that Rev. Wildmon deplores. He is hot on the trail of such scenes as this. Never will it be allowed in our domain, he says, tossing another book into the fire like my last wife liked to do. She'd throw away anything that didn't go with the wallpaper. Wildmon is another homegrown idiot from the state of Mississippi. Now he's gone totally nuts, as most preachers with a political cause do. He has attacked Mighty Mouse for sniffing cocaine to get his strength. The cartoon Mighty Mouse was a loser anyway, like a flying Jimmy Bakker. He just glanced around. My wife beckons me back with her arms to our bed after all these nights away from her. I blame myself for being an artist and how awful it must be to miss me.

⬛ ⬛

Yelverston's boy was not a genius but he had his own way. He grew up and went to college and found the one he loved. The river pirates killed him for his tape deck. His wife was reaching toward his poor dying body to save him and they blew her hand off. He and his wife were camping under some willows with their twelve-foot boat pulled up on the bank. They had been catching a few fish in the Tennessee–Tombigbee waterway. The dope pirates were all black, but led by a white wino from Texas named Coresta Haim. The murder was so vicious and unreasonable it could only be compared to the wild murders of the Harp brothers back in the early days of the Natchez Trace. These blacks were a new ruthless breed in Mississippi and Alabama, who used crack and ran cocaine. Haim would sniff cocaine and direct them along the waterway as he drank his wine. He was a connoisseur of the vino. They would run a certain amount of powder and weed and then go back to Mobile and get more, and when they went back they were hungover and bored. That's when they saw the Yelverston couple.

Yelverston and his wife joined with the sheriffs along the river and brought the crew to justice. It was an amazing story of vengeance and righteous diligence in investigation. They rounded up every one of them. Now they're all in Parchman prison and Yelverston has remarried his first wife.

❏ ❏

Yelverston took his wife down to Key West.

He was an old American, sixty-two, and Ruth was fifty. But she could still conceive and she was far away from her "change of life."

They had taken contraceptive measures.

Personally, I wish him well. I have too many children already. There is a quality of life when you listen to all of Bach and some jazz and you are out of cigarettes. Nobody is left but your pretty blond wife. Everything has been shut out.

They went to Key West and stayed in an apartment next to Louie's Backyard. They were astounded by the changes in Key West, with all the queers and the girls baring their breasts on the sailboats and the well-built gay men with their bathing suits like black jockstraps showing off all their butts. They waded in the water and swam toward the sailboats and they had punch system on the radio in case they had to work at the hospital or they had to rush in and suck a dick. Yelverston's wife held one of the punch buttons while a slim queer with a mustache went out swimming in his jockstrap.

Yelverston had been out to Big Pine Key fishing for bonefish and permit with Bill Schwicker. Bill had poled all over the bay and Yelverston had hung a five-foot lemon shark for fifteen seconds on a light Daiwa reel outfit with a floating crab. It was a thrill and he saw the fellow out there hung and resenting it. It snapped the line. The bay in the shallows of Big Pine Key was extremely clear and green-white right to the bottom. They ran up on a big nurse shark that was so big Yelverston didn't see it until the boat was almost over it and then it was there, purple-brown and about a foot across and it moved and Yelverston saw it. Why should this thing live when his son was dead? He watched it go out and struggle in the shallow water eating the little crustaceans out of the sand. Why should the niggers and the Texan still live in Parchman? They were all on death row now but Yelverston decided to change that. He decided to get them out of jail and own them. He no longer feared his own death. Death was nothing, death was the least of his worries. His son was dead but here was he with his handsome head of gray hair and his Pall Malls, five a day, and his habit of having five drinks a day, even though he had developed an ulcer. He realized he was an old fart and he and his wife had listened to old fart music coming down to Key West. His teeth needed fixing, his ulcer needed fixing. But just a swim in the crystal waters of Key West set him back on the track, and his mind cleared. He wanted to own one of the killers. He wanted to work him and train him until he was a close friend.

He saw the sun setting out in the Tortugas and realized that there was no revenge. There was never any revenge. He had been hitting them with a smile for years. Now his smile was tired and when he got home he saw his ex-wife, new wife, naked, lying on the couch innocently watching Wimbledon tennis. He was thinking about everything in the world. But he got naked too and the air conditioning rushing in felt wonderful after the hot trip with a sun around 97 degrees, and his head getting sunsick, so that he needed a couple of aspirins. He was wandering in his brain and wishing to die to be alongside his son in the grave. He was wishing to lie down with all the cool dead from all centuries. He was that tired. But his wife looked good and he wanted her. So she leaned over the bed and he gave her pleasure for ten minutes and he had his pleasure with her. He had almost forgotten how quiet and sweet her breasts with the big nipples were. He regarded the vagina where he had placed his son and saw it as a miracle of anatomy. He had never seen completely what a miracle the vagina was with his wife's white behind and her long tanned legs and brown toes spread on the floor. He wanted to do it again and now her hair was gray but she backed up on him and tossed her rump around like a girl. His heart was beating very fast and he lay on the couch, hoping he would have a heart attack that would take him off instantly to the town where his son lived. But he loved giving joy to his wife and she was lying in her robe taking a nap now too. What a thing it was to have a woman like this with his come in her and her being a woman around him, straightening the kitchen and bitching about small things. How he'd missed it!

Theories of women have gone around a while.

At one point Yelverston read all of them — Freud, Jung, and Miriam Fast, who conjoined all the information ever submitted about women on a computer and prescribed that most women want a glass of white wine on the rocks and a hard member underwater in a cool ocean inlet near the mangroves in Florida and a hundred thousand to shop with. He'd listened to the lesbians on teevee. They were mentioning how enlarged the world would be without men. If only they could just bite each other's carpet and think of releasing delinquent young women now in prison but soon to go out and kill men. His wife had a smile on her now as she slept. Women invent the special lovely things of the world, and have an elevated regard for the "mundane" and a deep driven sense like a seventh sense that they are the mama lions and they will protect all their cubs even if it means killing the papa. Okay?

His wife awoke grinning and told him she was dreaming of deer in a green meadow with high yellow flowers in it. She said she was running naked with the deer and she was as fast as they were, so fast that she began flying. She could feel the wind whipping by her bare feet and she put her legs behind her like a bird. She was leading the deer to a watering place. The big eyes of the does and the stags were watching me, she told Yelverston. Then we all came down and got in the water and the deer and I went underwater but it was just like a space full of diamonds and all we had to do was breathe in the blue air with diamonds twinkling around us. Then we got in a substance that was water and air and food all together. Then I woke up and I've just never felt better, honey, she told him.

Oh, Ruth.

He wanted her again and she obliged him. He knew he was a monster but he had to take her in the mouth this time and then come on her big generous breasts with the nipples dripping. Why do men need this? Yelverston asked himself. To make an elegant woman like her with her dreams of deer submit to this and degrade her? He thanked her. No, she said, thank you, darling. I've never done this for any other man, she said.

He was so amazed he slept.

He himself went into a dream where he was with his son and the lad was smiling as he walked on water.

I miss my sons now, one in Nashville, one in Tuscaloosa. I miss my daughter Lee too. They are all safe and I pray for them in their cars and traffic. Susan misses her son David every day. He is in Easley, South Carolina, with his pop and stepmother. He has more advantages up there in the foothills of the Blue Ridge Mountains. For the most part it is just my wife and I together in the gray house hating each other and then going into a coma when the television from Memphis takes over. She falls asleep and I try to slip out and get next to strange nooky but she always wakes up and tracks me down in her gown and bedroom slippers. I have had so much young nooky on my arm telling them about what a famous writer I am, but my wife shows up screaming in the alley like a fishwife, her blond hair flying around her face, and it's over. I try to get nooky at Square Books while the classical music is going and the doughheads with slumping shoulders wearing black socks with black hightop sneakers are standing around trying to remember their own names. Richard Howorth has the best bookstore in the South, but how come you never see any long-legged classical nooky in there? Does literature of fine quality only invite the ugly and the weird and the confident brilliant idiots who are writing things called The World As We Know It on endless legal pads? I go up there and have my cup of cappuccino, pretending to give a damn about *The New York Times Book Review*, but mainly wanting a lit-crazed nurse in white garter belt and white spike heels to light my cigarette and lick my face. You never see somebody like her to discuss feminism with. Three months ago I heard the rumor that women have feelings too, and I want to talk about it.

Women are the great new business to man every day. Every day. It goes without saying that a woman with good legs in sandals beats the hell out of a greasy breakfast with grits and comments about money. A woman who is not a swamp in a dress is a brilliant mystery, says I. And maybe Yelverston.

We *rely* on women the rest of our lives, said Yelverston. He was going down to see his daughter-in-law with her poor missing right hand. Then he told me some more.

❑ ❑

A terrible thing happened when Ron Shapiro's dog King got run over. King was always in the Hoka, wanting some petting. He was a black dog ten years old who leapt beautifully for a Frisbee. The guy who hit him near the railroad underpass called in and said he was to blame for the death of King. None of us wanted King ever to go. But he did. So canny about cars before, maybe he had got old and couldn't dart away anymore. Maybe he was tired of the same old trips back and forth to the Hoka, to Willie Morris's house. Down at Key West, Yelverston told me, they let the dogs swim in the ocean. He watched the dogs, all stripes and breeds, wade out and swim and walk on the sandbars. The noble sincere faces of dogs have always touched me deeply, as they have Yelverston. King would go out to the sandbars and ask, Are you coming along with me? Then he would stand up with his black hair all wet and ask us, What next, Masters? Every clod lost diminishes the continent, as John Donne said. David Holman is gone, an expert at literature, and King is gone, an expert at black dog. We are not the same without them.

❏ ❏

Yelverston and his wife drove through the Everglades and they went through the "Indian villages" and on the airboats through the brown glades in the swamps. Good thing to have a tank of gas going through the Everglades. For three hours there was nothing but the canals and the glades, and the Indian villages. His wife became amazingly bitter and angry out here in the sun-drenched nowhere with all the Indian history, Osceola and the boys. Even in the air-conditioned Jaguar sedan with the phone in it, she became bitter and began blaming Yelverston for the traits in their son which had come from Yelverston and led to the boy's murder. Your damned belief that people are kind and reasonable!

Your damned optimism about the earth being your friend! They stopped at an Indian village and Yelverston paid for an airboat ride. He'd never been on one of these contraptions, although he'd sold and bought boats of all sorts all over the world. The driver was a scrawny jerk who was maybe Seminole by way of a generation of petty thieves. He had a filthy gasoline-smelling aqua-blue blouse on him and deeply pitted skin. But his long black hair was handsome, tied behind him in a pigtail, screwing down his hunched back. The airboat got off faster than Yelverston thought it would, and he could see in the kid's eyes that he wanted to scare Yelverston and his wife and make one of them howl for a slower pace. But his wife said nothing and he said nothing, holding onto the gunnels for the ride and despising each other. Her dress flew up in her face and Yelverston saw her fine suntanned legs and her encouraging sandals. He wanted her, all in the speed and even as he hated her so much. They went over the weeds at 50 mph.

They went past alligators, who were just lying around, enormous, being prehistoric, sleepy, totally horny when the season came on, victims of tides and any asshole with a lantern and a high-powered rifle. All the wives and husbands and Texans waiting for the belts and the shoes. Yelverston looked at his wife's sandals and they were made of lizard skin. They dismounted the boat and went ahead in cold silence, despising each other, then went into the Indian hut where people sold everything that looked charmed and natural from the region. He saw his wife looking at a necklace of silver and stones and he saw the peace in her eyes suddenly and he knew all the ugliness was out of her. The speed on the airboat had caught up with her and the recriminations had flown away. The same thing had happened to him. His useless pity for all things killed and disgraced went through the hot air and down the white man's highway and on into St. Petersburg, through the hordes of stores and the billboards that Florida had become. A horror of "For Sale." You run through Florida from Key West to Point Clear, Alabama, and you don't even meet human Southern courtesy until you get to a gas station run by blacks in north St. Petersburg. The man who raises the hood has a toothache. The girl who owns the place is trying to make it congenial. Even when Yelverston's wife was bitchy, the black girl with her sincerity won her over. "Please have a safe journey," the girl said.

In upper Florida, where boiled peanuts were sold in a bar and the people were kind, the anger finally broke. They took an old motel with separate cottages as in the old days of the fifties and stayed in them till their anger was broken. Yelverston looked out through the folding glass and saw the rest of his neighbors around here. They were people who were there with wives and children in Chevy station wagons, people who could not afford to have a fight like this in the shade of the live oaks and under the Spanish moss, in a green oyster-shell-driveway kind of place. With a small swimming pool behind the restaurant, which was wood-paneled and had stuffed fish on the wall. Yelverston got naked and he began hating himself for being rich. He hated himself for running with his smart dreams and conquering everything. There was a time to turn over and be defeated, too, and be out of it and quit pretending to adore everybody he was in business with. There were so many weaselly little cowards he had commended because they gave him money and respect. He had quit smoking but he got a pack of salty old Pall Malls out of his kit. He had got them salty making love to his wife in the ocean five days ago. Sir Walter Raleigh, huh? he asked himself.

His wife was in the other cottage, and she told me later that she was distressed at what she had become, too. She had not armed her son with the canniness. She had not armed her son with the survivalness. He was too dumb and too smart. In the hospital, when she had seen her son's wife with her hand blown away, seen the lovely skinny girl with her missing hand bandaged and taken care of, she could not remember the girl's name. The girl started having a glow around her like a saint. Ruth's daughter-in-law's name was Grace Helen. She walked away, did Yelverston's wife. She was blinded by tears and so much wasted time that she had to see Yelverston immediately. He was in Oklahoma by that time, asking how to get back at the killers, how to find them all. Lloyd Helms was a sort of friend of his and he got all the Mississippi sheriffs on the line. Her womb was on fire to conceive another baby at the last of her time. She left her husband with a brief phone call and flew to Yelverston.

She finally found him at the funeral of their son. She addressed him and then she got nude. He did not want to make love but she got him out of his trousers and pressed her breasts against it. Come on, come on, she said. He couldn't but she persisted. Yes you can. I've read all the books about what you men want, she said.

❑ ❑

At the best of my trumpet playing and my poetry writing there occurred a wonderful young lady named Tidy Armstrong from Rolling Fork, Mississippi. She had been taken by two athletes on the Choctaw team and I knew it. She had had her virginity taken away twice violently, but she was disappointed. We met there under the cedars near the Old Chapel where Grant had stabled his horses and attacked Vicksburg. She was smoking Salems and she handed me one but I'd quit for the last two months because I thought my future lay with my trumpet. I was still rather tiny but sincere. My limbs did not fill out my shirt or pants. Tidy told me: Please marry me. Don't marry her. Tears were coming out of her eyes.

———

We would have been divorced but we would have had respect for each other. Also she would have fought and died for our love. She would have never grown lazy and fat or mean. Where is Tidy now? Now that for me everything is as good as it will ever be. Like Yelverston and his wife—what was her name? Ruth—you can stumble ahead and bust through the next zone. Into the plenitude and into the horror. I look at all the movies and the teevee and the car wrecks and the explosions and the drugs and the antialcohol warnings from the rich hospitals and the ranks of phonies charging toward the old fart with a mere Gatling gun in the lighthouse, his mustache on fire. The old guys are me now, is the horror. I'll wander up and get registered and vote.

Jimmy Buffett came by the house the other day. He's lost some hair but he's looking great, very muscular and ready for his tour. Jimmy flies his plane to Belize with his sweetheart. Buffett is a sketch and we are all waiting on his next good tune. He has complete steel in his eyes. He can't spell and he has a café called Margaritaville in Key West on Duval Street. Almost all the waiters have sandy blond hair like Jimmy. Jimmy once gave me $7500 for a title on a song, and then wrote a happy Las Vegas tune beneath it. His tribe will increase. There is a happiness and sincerity in Jimmy's best tunes that has touched us all.

Jimmy Buffett gave me hope in Tuscaloosa. He is smart as a whip with his old songs and they make you carry on. Do you realize the millions of Southerners who are ready to drop out and go to the Caribbean and sail to Jimmy's parents' house? J. D. and Peets? What lovely people. She always sends me a note at Christmas. And Laurie and Tom McGuane, what people. I was never in any "extended family" around any of them, but Tom lent me money when I was low and he was surprised when I paid him back. He is a champion at everything. In Montana, I saw him knock three clay pigeons out of the air on Thanksgiving Day, hitting them from three directions with no long sweat. Laurie, beautiful brunette. She cooks and she exercises and she has gotten exalted, though people who mess around with horses over the years get strange on you. They amaze the little people like me. They spend immense sums to keep their keenness going. They have no demeaning job and so they buy jobs and hard problems. But they are the cavaliers, baby, and we need them. Tom McGuane was never from Michigan. He was a Virginia cavalier when he was born. God bless him and his books, and his brunette Laurie.

The fact, however, is: I have shelter, nooky, and respect. I have no complaints. I hate my wife, but she still keeps coming back. Even when she has the cramps and I'm out of money she cheers me. She says I am her hero. Even when she hates me she knows I'm her hero. I've fought in no wars, unlike the great calm Quisenberry who goes through his separation from Kathy in California like a piece of granite. I was out in the pasture fighting like hell as a tiny sincere guy but the Quisenberrys knew that to be cool and smart was the right way to be.

2000

The great publisher Sam Lawrence moves down to the South with his lovely lady Joan Williams. Sam was trying to keep up with McGuane and Jim Harrison for a while, according to his housekeeper Liz Lear. He was drinking and smoking and sniffing for a while. That's why Sam Lawrence is beloved to me. He is a golden man, flying to there and thither. All over the planet for his authors. He comes to see his authors and gives them spirit. Comes in a stretch limo to my humble house and makes the darkies at the icehouse stretch their necks. Nothing like that had ever occurred in Oxford, Mississippi. We've promised the moon to each other, Sam and I. We'll get the little ball down here sitting like a tame cool thing in our laps, domestic as a big flashlight. All the generations of wonderful dead guys behind us. All the Confederate dead and the Union dead planted in the soil near us. All of Faulkner the great. Christ, there's barely room for the living down here. We lost the war but we lost in such a wonderful way that even the blacks still look at us with awe. I'm free, boss, but would you give me a cigarette? I've personally been beaten so many times that death looks like a pussy to me. Come on, little dude, show me something. I've spoken my head off in nine books and have twenty lovers and friends behind me. Sam Lawrence will move next to me and be my Dutch uncle and we will cure each other of our diseases until the little bitch death shows up.

BOOMERANG

The last time I threw the boomerang was on the dirty beach of Biloxi, Mississippi. This time I had a black fiber-glass model that cost five dollars. The price hasn't gone up since 1952 that much I guess because there hasn't been a great demand and nobody except an aborigine in Australia knows how to use them. My wife and her children had got me a little terrier for Christmas. I'd named her Ruth, as *Ruth* married to Yelverston. Shannon and David were around the oak trees and they released the little dog to me, and she ran toward me with her white-and-black body coming forward like my old fox terrier Honey in the old days at this house, the home of my parents Bill and Elizabeth.

We took Ruth down to Biloxi and I threw the boomerang out in the gray cold late afternoon. We'd been having some fights and misunderstandings during the winter. There were no sea gulls to aim at or even harass. The weather was bad, the light was awful, the water was brown and rolling in reluctantly, the motel was cheap, the month was February. I just felt we had a need to be here by the ocean with our dog Ruth, the little black-and-white terrier got out of the Jackson Animal Rescue League.

My wife leaned on me, trying not to hate me. I threw the boomerang and this one acted amazingly. It took off seventy yards or so and then came back higher and much lazier. It was spinning in this beach grayness and taking its time, extremely patient to come back, hovering out there and seeming to inch toward us directly back to my hand.

I held my hand out as stunned as I was. It came in so easy and catchable I closed my fist.

Little Ruth, the dog, caught it behind me in her jaws. She just saw it and leapt up and there the big thing was in her happy mouth. She ran down the beach with it.

❑ ❑

Went up to Square Books and got the *New York Times*, read about some poor Yugoslav bastard who was in Siberia for having a wrong thought or something. For twenty years. For twenty fucking years. For *twenty* years. Now he's come out with his statement that it was bad and that all he thought about was survival.

*

Yesterday was July Fourth. The Russians and their history. Vietnam and its history. They kill their mothers and fathers by the millions.

I love the land of the free. I'm standing on soil full of blood and I am still stealing from *me*. Even me, smart, and I've gotten away with it.

When I get tired of my wife I can dance.

I can work at the old Smith-Corona she gave me for Father's Day.

I can take my friends fishing and act like an important person. Blasting snakes out of the water with my pump twenty gauge. Catching bass from Mr. Latham King's farm pond. Bringing home the food, fresh from the waters of North Mississippi.

FURTHERANCE

When they got back to Mississippi, Yelverston could not even remember his wife's name, he was so drunk. She was so good-looking to him and they were in some Hilton or something in Jackson, Mississippi, a town which was really dumb. Yelverston chuckled. Even Larry Speakes can get over them here. Noteworthy about the Reagan administration was that even Larry Speakes, a man who was born to do judgments on the height of rodeo manure, could write a book. These are the awfullest of all times, thought Yelverston.

He could not remember his wife's name, but she was in her red silk pajamas. She was fifty but she wanted his baby. She took off her panties and assisted him. She was a lovely woman and he plunged into her.

Ruth!

All his wonderful memories of everything shot

into her womb and in nine months they had a new baby.

His name was Carl.

P.S.

Throughout the hate and the temporary madnesses, and the envies and the lack of regard and the calamities that have occurred and all the deaths that have happened as given to us by the mad U.S.A. and the mad god, Yelverston has kept on.

I visited him in Mobile for a while with his wife Ruth, but then he had to move up to Memphis because his heart was not doing well with that much heat and humidity in it. Personally, I know the difference. I visited Point Clear, Alabama, recently, with my brother Bobby and his wife Grace. Even at nine in the morning the breath was coming so heavy to my lungs it had already cut me down. Had to get in my air-conditioned Chrysler LeBaron with my wonderful wife, named Susan, who was born in 1946 but will not die yet, so as I can go on and be her tormentor and so that we will have our neighbors Stuart Cole and Bryan who provide speakers for the bingo and who meet with me at three A.M. and we share music. Tonight I'm listening to "Chariots of Fire" and the Christian in me goes on and goes on, even where the others let down, I get in training with my espresso, my Light Winstons, my friends.

Chariots of Fire was the last movie my mother and

I saw together. We got together, finally, on one point when we watched it together.

In this, my third marriage, there is a way to keep living. Work hard four days and cut off three. My wife takes the phone off the hook and I lie in bed in our new king-size bed with all the animals in bed around me. Nellie the cat since Iowa, Joseph the Lhasa apso from Arkansas, Missy the dog from the Jitney Jungle and Mr. Levi, whose daughter Alice was jubilant and kind to us.

Carl, the new manager at Kroger's, who was wearing his smart madras tie today in the Gin, is a good Alabama guy. I meet the good people from everywhere here in Oxford — the cream of the crop. I've got my madras coat.

Took my wife to the hospital tonight with a migraine. She's got PMS and took Cafergot with phenobarb in it, but it didn't obtain. Bryan, next-door neighbor, took us to the emergency room.

In the emergency room with her migraines and her PMS, we met with good people. An old guy with a cane and a good sweater whose wife had a brain hemorrhage. We prayed for his wife. He was a bootlegger and chief of police and worked with the FBI and was a veteran of the island fights in World War Two.

I and Bryan gave a prayer for the old man's wife. One day all of us will have to have a brain hemorrhage and be flown off to Baptist Hospital in Memphis in a helicopter. For all the bad I've said about the Baptists, some of them have a good hospital.

Certain guys you cannot stop from being good even though they have zero money. Dr. Cooper establishes a mission in Mexico. Dr. Guy goes to Honduras to help the animals. The good love is flooding from this little town and we need the encouragement of Sam Lawrence's stretch limousine, we need all the encouragement we can get.

My wife was stoned on Nubane and the relief in her head was wonderful. She couldn't even stand up, and *then* she came into the living room where I work and wrote this note:

> I love you—thanks for being there—always. Please smile for me. Thanks for being my bestest friend. Would you still be my lover and knight in shiney armour. How terribly be withoutest I'd be without. Think of the lonliniss I'd much rather *(incomprehensible)* I'm your biggest fan *(totally unreadable)*.

On this drug she shouldn't have written anything at all but she wrote to say she loved me. Couldn't do without me.

Yelverston lives in a Memphis mansion very close to Shelby Foote, the great Civil War historian, and William Eggleston, the world-famous photographer. Which means he and I blast away at coins on a Sunday afternoon with our enormous collection of guns. Cowgirls are appearing to my mind. Somebody who would just graze me on the forehead with her handgun and then lift her skirts, showing thigh and boot.

Cut it down, babies. Cut it down all around the world. Quit shooting. Quit it, quit it, gallant Mississippians. Take time to write everybody a love note that you love. Take take take time to examine your own wife's anatomy and her clean clothes for you and take care of your children.

Yelverston brought young Carl on his arm to my little shack on Van Buren. His wife Ruth was very proud. Yelverston was wearing a beard now, very gray. He had on shorts and his legs were tanned. He was sixty-five years old now and Ruth was looking about forty, with her hair blond, but I knew she was much older. She must have had all the benefits.

Little Carl was running around the place.

My wife was in her best because we knew they were coming. She was in her high heels and the pink gown of immense expense. You get to be writer-in-residence at Ole Miss and you don't mess around anymore. Your wife has the best clothes and you meet only the best people.

There was a guy coming up the concrete stairs, a humble-looking man in a good brown suit. I had no idea what to say. He looked important but a little pale.

"Susan Hannah," my wife said.

"Coresta Haim," he said.

There was a big pause when I and my wife recognized the white man with sweat on his brow.

We had the best wine out and turkey and ham and mushroom salad. It was a hundred degrees and the air conditioners were on full blast.

"This is the man who killed my son," Yelverston said to me. "I think he'll want some wine."

Ruth and Susan got on very well. Little Carl was a horror, a loud running two-year-old.

Yelverston lent me $3000 on the condition that I quit smoking and Susan and I have a baby.

They left. We'd been talking about what the Civil War was about.

Yelverston got very drunk and lit one Pall Mall after the other. Coresta Haim sat on the other end of the couch with me.

"Barry, I had millions at one time, but I was nothing," Haim told me.

Yelverston looked around at me. He had a suit I'd never seen before. His belt was purple. His wife was in the next room, and she was beautiful, tanned. I had Bach on the stereo. Yelverston went and shut off the music. Then he cut all the lights off. All the air conditioning stopped and it was black and nobody said a word.

"I didn't die yet," Yelverston said. "None of us have died yet."

The medical news has come in.
It's all good.

After three years of trying my wife and I have a new baby coming too. What a lie. We have nothing coming.

We have Oxford and our friends, maybe, all in line, making a defense around Oxford so as to keep the carpetbaggers out.

November 10, '88.

Willie Morris's movie *Good Old Boy* premiered at the Hoka. We all had on tuxedos and the women were in their dresses and serious patrician shoes and splendid earwear. Yelverston and Ruth were there. He'd come back from his heart condition. He'd quit drinking and smoking altogether and told me he was miserable but now he was an old man and his wife liked him a lot better. It was a tender movie about youth in Yazoo City. When they played taps for the fallen man at the little cemetery, I started crying a little. Sitting next to me was Ruth Yelverston, with her smart white skirt and her wonderful legs reaching down to her black slim high heels. She was tearing up too and I lent her my handkerchief.

"You know, Barry," she whispered in my ear,

"Willie's movie's so wonderful, about when you were young and it was almost all fun, with nature and the friendly darkies all around you. I'm so sorry I'm sick."

They went away and when I was counting all the money for the Humane Society, Cor Haim, the man who murdered Yelverston's son, touched me on the elbow. He added five thousand-dollar bills to the fund. He smiled at me, in his tux. The Hoka, when the film was shown, was all around us—the plank walls, the tin roof, the reggae and blues posters on the wall, the endless nobility of females in their gowns and earrings.

"Ruth's gone with cancer. Got maybe seven months," he said.

"That's not possible," I just about shouted at him. Then I cut my voice down. "That's not possible. Look how she looks, look how she's—" I looked at her in the television lights. They were interviewing her under the lights and she, in her gray hair parted in the middle, was the belle of the ball.

Yelverston was there with his little son. He was smiling and handsome. A couple of black chauffeurs came in to handle them.

"Those are two of the guys who actually shot his son and his daughter-in-law."

I looked at Cor Haim.

"He rehabilitated them," said Haim. "Or thinks he did."

*

We, I and Yelverston, put Ruth in the ground this spring.

In a mansion in Memphis, he has the blacks and Cor Haim around him, taking care of Carl.

It's a lifetime deal, he tells me.